Rescued by a Prince

A Novel

Ginny Hartman

First printing: December 2016

ISBN-13: 978-1541021563

To Dad,
the man who knows how to do it all
and does it all so well.
You're my hero.

Prologue

The distant sound of a horse galloping encroached upon her thoughts as Rose knelt next to the small flower patch in front of the cottage, enthusiastically digging in the dirt. She was determined to get something to grow there besides the tangled weeds that had overtaken it after several years of neglect.

Brushing her hands on her skirt, she quickly rose as the pounding of the horse's feet grew closer. Retreating towards the door of the cottage, she couldn't help but look around, her eyes wide with curiosity as she waited to see what was going on. She had been living at the cottage for nearly a month, and during that time she had seen no one except her lady's maid who was her only companion in her new life.

"Infernal beast."

Rose felt alarm course through her at the heated insult as a man atop a horse came into view, pulling to a quick stop. She began shaking as the man's hardened stare settled upon her. It was not the first time she had been called such a name, but since her husband's death, she had certainly hoped she would never hear such insults hurled in her direction again.

She stood rooted in her spot as the man slid from atop his horse. She wanted to run inside the cottage and hide, but fear kept her frozen in place. It was as if she was before her husband again, awaiting whatever punishment his anger demanded. She bit the inside of her cheek to keep from crying as her hands wrapped nervously around her skirt.

The man drew near, his long legs taking quick steps up the path. Rose flinched, her eyes closing so she would not have to see the look of anger she was certain would be on his face. Her breath stilled as she waited. The first blow was always the worst; she remembered that all too well. After the initial pain spread through her, a blessed numbing would overtake her, allowing her to withstand the assault.

She kept her eyes scrunched tightly together for several long seconds, anticipating the beating that she was certain would come. When nothing happened, she forced herself to open her eyes, to see if she had only just imagined the odd encounter.

"Good day, miss," the man muttered, but instead of sounding like a polite salutation, his voice tilted curiously making it seem as if he was asking her a question instead.

Oddly enough, her first desire was to correct the man and let him know she was a lady, not a miss, but she quickly tempered the notion down, knowing he wouldn't give a fig about her standing in society.

She was a nobody now, had been for quite some time.

When nothing but silence ensued, the man continued, "Are you well? I certainly did not mean to frighten you."

Rose could only manage to nod her head stiffly in response.

"I'm looking for my dog. The blasted hound got away from me again. Worthless hunting dog, if you ask me. Can't even stay by my side. The first unfamiliar noise and he's off. Have you perchance seen him?"

It took a moment for Rose to process that the man had been addressing his hound earlier and not her, that he hadn't come to harm her after all. Slowly, her body quit shaking, and she allowed herself to look into the man's eyes for the first time. His eyes were green, she noted, but not a magnificent emerald green. They were more of a muted green, the color of light moss, and the way he was staring at her caused an unfamiliar chill to sweep down her spine.

His gaze was so intent, so filled with concern that she wanted to weep. She was not used to a man looking at her with anything other than disdain. Unless of course, she counted her brother Griffin, but his look was usually one of pity mixed with an inordinate amount of brotherly love.

"I...uh, I..." she stammered as she quickly looked away from his intense stare and back towards the cottage.

The man chuckled lowly, causing her insides to heat. What was it about this man's presence that caused such strange reactions? "I must apologize for my sudden appearance, for I can see I have unnerved you, miss." He offered her his hand, which she gingerly took, embarrassed by the dirt smudges that marred her ivory skin. He bowed before her, her hand still in his, before rising. She hadn't realized just how tall he was until that moment. "I am Cameron deCourtenay. My father is the Marquess of Hilldale. Our property is not far from here."

She stood for a moment taking in his appearance, from his windswept brown hair to his powerful jawline and admitted to herself that he was easily the most handsome man she had ever seen. Just his nearness was making her speechless.

Pulling her hand swiftly from his grasp, she found herself muttering in a small voice, "I'm Miss Ivison, and no, I have not seen your dog." She wasn't exactly sure why she had given the man her maiden name, she only knew she never wanted to be affiliated with her late husband again.

He sighed in frustration as one hand ran anxiously through his hair. "Well do me a favor, miss. If you do by chance encounter the brute, go ahead and keep him. I'm confident he'd make a better lady's companion than he does a hunting dog. Good day."

Rose watched as he turned on his heel and stalked back to his horse. He mounted without another glance in her direction and was galloping off before she could judge whether he had been serious about the dog or not.

That night she dreamed she was a princess locked away in a tower by herself. Loneliness consumed her each waking minute, and she desperately wished someone would rescue her. It was a dream she often had, but this night was different, for she dreamed a rescuer did come, a gallant prince with muted green eyes and a velvety voice that could charm a flea off a dog.

"Everything will be alright," his voice cooed as he gathered her into his arms and made to escape.

Looking up into his handsome face she was struck with a jolt of awareness, for she believed him. She glanced down at her hands, hands that were covered in ugly, puckered scars and watched in amazement as they slowly began to fade. How was it possible that this man was able to make her scars dissolve so quickly when she had been trying to erase them for years without any success?

But alas, she would never know, for she was awoken at that moment by the incessant barking of a dog.

Rose groaned, hating to leave the dream she was having. Grabbing a wrapper off the trunk at the foot of her bed, she quickly slid into it before slipping from the cottage into the chilly night, hoping she could silence the hound before it woke her maid.

Still attempting to adjust her eyes to the darkness, Rose never saw the fluffy, black dog coming until it was upon her, knocking her on her backside on the walk. She had no time to worry if the dog was vicious before it was eagerly licking her face.

She laughed as her arms went around the big ball of fluff. "You are not an infernal beast at all, are you?" The dog, a Newfoundland, barked in response before resuming it's licking.

Using every ounce of strength she could muster, Rose stood and ushered the dog into the cottage. She would have to figure out a way to return the pup to Lord deCourtenay, for though he had told her to keep him, she knew she couldn't do it—the dog was nearly bigger than she was!

It soon became apparent, however, that there would be no returning the dog, for Rose had no way of finding the Earl and the dog seemed to have no desire to leave. She was secretly pleased, for the massive dog not only made her feel safe, but he also filled her life with purpose and gave her someone to think of beside herself. She named him Prince, for she had been dreaming of being rescued by a prince when he arrived, and she knew full well he might be the only prince she ever encountered in her lifetime.

Chapter One

The closest thing Rose ever felt to happiness was when she was snuggling her youngest nephew in her arms. Since he began walking recently, the only time she got to do that anymore was when he was asleep. Inhaling deeply of his soft baby scent, she nuzzled his cheek, careful not to wake him. It was a shame she would never get the opportunity to hold a child of her own. Her heart constricted painfully at the thought, but she had become an expert at tampering the overwhelming emotion, quickly dispelling it before it caused tears to well up in her eyes.

She was grateful that she had successfully willed herself not to cry when her sister-in-law, Adel came quietly into the nursery, smiling as she took in the scene before her. "Damien looks precious when he is asleep."

"He always looks precious, in my unbiased opinion."

1

Adel laughed softly. "As his favorite aunt, you are most definitely biased."

Rose's eyes widened with pleasure. "You are admitting I am his favorite?" Adel nodded, and her heart nearly burst, for she knew that Adel's only sister, Katherine, vied anxiously for the lofty position.

"But do not breathe a word to Katherine, you know how upset that would make her."

Rose gave her solemn vow. "She may not be Damien's favorite aunt, but I am certain Henry and Conrad prefer her. Especially since she has never scolded them for running through the drawing room with muddy feet."

Adel laughed as she thought of her two older sons. "They are lucky it was you who found them and not me, for they would have received a far worse scolding from their mother, I can assure you."

Rose wasn't sure how Adel did it. Her sons were the most rambunctious boys in all of England. She got tired just spending a few hours with them, let alone being responsible for their care day in and day out.

"Adel?" Rose asked slowly.

"Yes?"

"I think I'm ready for a change." Adel paused, looking at her cautiously and Rose wanted to flinch. Why did she blurt that out just now? They had been talking about her nephews, not her future.

Without saying a word, Adel gently scooped Damien from her arms and laid him softly in his cradle before indicating that Rose follow her. Rose twisted her hands in her skirts nervously as she did as her sister-in-law bid, her heart beating rapidly as her nerves threatened to overcome her. She had been contemplating discussing her future with Adel and her brother Griffin for some time now, but when she awoke that morning, she had not planned on today being the day. In all actuality, she wasn't certain she was ready to do so now, but it was too late to retract her words.

Once in the privacy of the drawing room, Adel turned to Rose excitedly. "I've been waiting for this moment for a long time now."

Rose startled at her admission. "You have?"

"Yes," Adel squealed, unconcerned about who may hear. "I've been patiently waiting for you to tire of that boring old cottage in the country and decide you were ready to have a season."

"Wait just a moment," she exhaled in alarm. "I most certainly did not mean to imply that I wanted to participate in the season. I was thinking more along the lines of seeking a post as a nanny. You see how much I adore Damien and since I will never have children of my own, I thought it would be a splendid way to fill that hole in my heart."

Adel looked at her bemusedly. "You know Griffin will never agree to that."

Rose sagged against the back of her chair. Her brother was more protective of her than Prince was of his only bone. "Perhaps you can convince him?" she asked with the faintest of hope.

Flashing one of her brilliant smiles, Adel shook her head slowly as auburn curls bounced about her face. "Even I do not hold that much sway over Griffin."

Rose knew that was not true. Her brother and Adel had been married almost four years, and in that time, she had never seen Griffin more besotted. "Could you at least ask?"

Adel was thoughtful for a moment before her face turned serious as she spoke. "Rose, I want nothing more than to see you happy, and I fear being holed up by yourself in the country is not the means to that end."

"I'm not alone," she quickly defended. "My lady's maid is a most excellent companion, as is Prince."

Adel rolled her eyes. "Let me remind you that you would never find a post as a nanny with that infernal beast as part of the deal."

Rose smiled, recalling Lord deCourtenay describing the dog in the same manner, all those years ago. Everyone seemed to think Prince was nothing but a nuisance, a very large nuisance at that, but she adored him. He had been her best friend for the last four years, and the thought of going anywhere without him was too dreadful to bear.

Adel interrupted her musings. "Do you wish to share the remainder of your days with only your lady's maid and Prince?"

"No, but that is why I often venture to London to be with your family."

"Rose, I've been thinking about it for quite some time now, and I believe you are ready."

"Ready for what?" trepidation laced each word, for she was certain she didn't want to hear what Adel thought her ready for.

"I think it's time you allowed yourself to fall in love."

Rose inhaled sharply as one hand went to her chest. Love is

something she knew nothing about. Sure, she had been wed before, for two horrendous years to be exact, but love had never, ever been part of the equation. In fact, her husband, the late Baron Moncreif, had treated her with such abuse, she was uncertain she ever wanted to be involved with another man again. The thought of being wed to another monster frightened her beyond reason.

When she failed to respond, Adel continued, "You once told me how you regretted the fact that you would never have the chance to know what true love was."

"I was married then," she whispered shakily, remembering the conversation well.

"And there was nothing to be done with those dreams. But Lord Moncreif has been dead nearly four years now. I think it's time you laid his memory to rest for good and find someone to make memories with that will replace all the horrible ones you have from the past."

"It's not as easy as all of that."

"It doesn't have to be complicated, Rose. People fall in love every day. If we begin at once, we can have a new wardrobe commissioned and everything ready before the opening of the season."

Adel's excitement was contagious, but trepidation still filled her breast. "I never got to have my first season," she confessed sadly.

"I know, and that is precisely why I am set on you having one now. Every woman of the *ton* should get to experience balls and soirees, dressed in the loveliest of dresses. It's about time you learned what it feels like to be adored, to be courted by the most handsome men in England."

"I wouldn't even know what to do with the attention."

"You're charming, Rose. All you have to do is be yourself and the men will adore you."

"I'm not so certain about that."

"Certain about what?"

Both women's eyes darted towards the door as Griffin's large frame filled the room. Adel beckoned him to her side then took his hand eagerly into her own. "Rose is ready to experience a London season."

Griffin nearly choked as his dark eyes found her own. "Am I hearing my wife correctly? Do you indeed desire to participate in the season?"

Feeling suddenly self-conscious, Rose stood, her eyes downcast as she muttered, "It's a silly idea, really."

"It is not silly." Adel was quick to come to her defense. "It's a splendid idea, and nothing you can say will change that, Griffin."

"Do you truly think it wise to throw her to the wolves?" His voice was rough, but that didn't conceal the concern behind his statement.

"You make it sound dreadful when you know it doesn't have to be like that. Not all men are like you and your dim-witted friends. I am certain there will be plenty of lovely gentlemen perfectly enamored with Rose."

Ignoring his wife, he pleaded with Rose, "What is wrong with the cottage? I thought you liked it there."

"I do."

"She does."

Both women answered at once.

"Then why do you suddenly find the urge to leave?"

"Griffin," Adel struggled to keep her patience. "Rose is a woman."

"I can see that," he growled.

"A woman who desires to fall in love."

"That's not precisely what I said," she interjected, but neither Adel nor Griffin seemed to hear her.

"Look, sweetheart, if you don't allow her to participate in the season, she has sworn to go find a post as a nanny."

"Certainly not," he roared, his face turning red. "You are a lady of quality Rose, not someone's employee."

"Lower your voice, Griffin. Damien is sleeping."

"In the nursery on the third floor," he bellowed loudly. "I don't know what either one of you is up to, but why, all of a sudden, do things have to change? Can't you be content with the way things are?"

Rose glanced between Griffin and Adel, desperately hoping Adel would come to her rescue. Silence ensued, and it was growing more and more uncomfortable by the moment.

Finally, Rose realized she'd have to defend herself. Squaring her shoulders, she looked directly into her brother's eyes. "How would you feel if things were reversed? If it was you who was living alone in a cottage in the country? How would you feel if nothing noteworthy had happened to you in the past four years? No marriage to Adel, no babies, nothing but the same thing day in and day out with no chance of anything ever changing. Ever."

"But—"

Exhibiting uncommon force, Rose stopped him by raising one

dainty hand in front of her. "I'm not suggesting I participate in the season to fall in love; I'm only looking for a diversion from my melancholy, and if I find a suitable husband then so be it."

Adel surprised them both by standing and applauding. "Bravo, Rose. I've been waiting for you to stand up for yourself for ages. Doesn't she make you proud, Griffin?"

"No dear, she makes me concerned. This is not the same Rose I have become accustomed to."

Rose's shoulders sagged. "Griffin, don't you remember how I used to be?" Her eyes searched his hopefully, "before I was forced to wed Lord Moncreif?"

"That seems so long ago," he replied sadly.

"Yes, because it was. I can hardly remember that girl myself, but some things I will never forget."

"Like what?"

"Like how happy I used to be and how I used to love a good adventure. There isn't much adventure to be found at the cottage."

"And you think you'll find adventure in a ballroom?"

"Griffin!" Adel exclaimed, "You are missing the point. The point is she is ready for a change, and I am more than willing to help her, with or without your permission."

Griffin threw his head into his hands and sighed. "Fiend seize it, when you set your mind to something, there's nothing I can do to stop you."

Adel beamed proudly. "Things will turn out splendidly, just you wait and see."

Rose returned her smile but with much less confidence. Something inside of her told her that perhaps she was placing herself in quite the predicament.

Chapter Two

"Ever heard of Lady Rose Moncreif?"

Cameron was thoughtful for a moment before shaking his head. His memory was impeccable, and he was positive he had never met, nor heard of the lady.

"She is the Baron Moncreif's widow. Lord Moncreif had an obsession with gambling but he rarely, if ever, won. He ran up debts all over London before the gossip columns started reporting of his misfortune. The man couldn't tolerate the shame and eventually killed himself."

"With all due respect, sir, it's not an uncommon tale."

"No, it's not," Andrew exhaled slowly.

Cameron sat patiently waiting for the man to come to the point. He knew he hadn't been summoned to the Main Office to discuss the unfortunate demise of some already forgotten Baron.

"We have reason to suspect that Lady Moncreif is involved in a string of murders that have taken place over the last four years since her husband's death. Our contact has recently informed us that she has decided to participate in the Season and mingle with society for the first time since his passing. This is where you come in."

Cameron leaned forward, listening intently to what he had to say. Truth be told, he had been nearly giddy with excitement since being summoned to the Main Office, for the prospect of going through an entire season without the distraction of an assignment had been truly upsetting to him.

"The common thread in each murder is that the victim had won a large sum of money from Lord Moncreif. It would appear these are crimes bent on retribution."

"And you suspect Lady Moncreif is behind them?" he asked with a bit of skepticism.

Andrew shrugged his shoulders. "She lost everything as a result of his gambling. I can't imagine she is pleased with the circumstance her late husband has left her in."

"What is it you need from me?"

Inspecting a piece of parchment on the desk in front of him, he continued, "We have determined, to the best of our abilities, every person who has ever won a significant amount from the Baron. We have reason to suspect that General Howe could be one of her next victims."

Cameron's shoulders stiffened, understanding full well the urgency in the assignment. "Does General Howe know?"

"Yes, and I can assure you that extra precaution has been taken to ensure his safety. What we need from you is to find out if Lady Moncreif is indeed guilty of these crimes so she can be stopped."

"Understood, sir."

"Do you need any further information?"

"No," he stated confidently. "I will find out what I need to know."

"And you will be discreet?"

He looked across the desk at the man, insulted by his question. "Am I ever anything but?"

"Of course not, but be careful lest you place your life in jeopardy as well."

Cameron made to leave, "I'm quite certain my life isn't that valuable to you."

The man smirked. "But keeping my job is. I've been on this case for three years, and this is the first break we have had. Don't ruin this for me."

"I won't," he said arrogantly as he waltzed from the room.

Cameron left the Main Office with a sense of excitement swirling inside of him. He lived for these assignments. He had worked as an agent during the war and White Hall had continued to summon him to be of service when needed. He was the perfect candidate for a secret agent too. Society saw him as the nothing more than the Earl of deCourtenay, the mysterious bachelor who refused to wed, but little did they know that he was one of the best agents in all of England. His duplicity amused him. The *ton* was expert at seeing only what they wanted to.

Returning to the study in his townhouse, he steepled his fingers together as he stared absently at the Chinese paper on the walls. He traced the red and gold pattern with his eyes as he thought. Most agents were given a missive containing information about the case they were assigned to, but the Main Office knew Cameron better than that. He didn't need a list of facts and he certainly did not like being responsible for the confidential information. Everything he needed to know, he would learn on his own and store it in his head where things never got forgotten or placed into the wrong hands.

If Lady Moncreif was indeed resurfacing in society this season, he was certain he could find out quite a bit of information at his club. The men who frequented White's were notorious for gossiping about the latest on dits of the *ton* perhaps even more than the women of London's drawing rooms were. Glancing at the clock on the mantle, he realized he had enough time for a nap before he would need to make his appearance at White's. Foisting himself from his chair, he retired to his bedchamber. He wanted to make sure he was well rested for the task ahead.

***

Though he preferred a booth tucked away in the corner, Cameron forced himself to sit at a table in the middle of all the bustle of people filing into White's. He needed to be privy to whatever information he could gather. Ordering a brandy, he sat back in his chair and observed the people around him as he silently tuned into the conversations going on all around him.

Most people believed him to be quiet because they supposed he had

14

nothing to say. What they didn't realize was, more often than not, he was busy listening and observing every detail that was going on around him. His intellect was keen, though most people thought him rather simple-minded. It amused him that the observation of his character could be so far off the mark.

Several minutes passed as he gathered nothing but petty gossip about some chit named Lady Violet. Nothing exciting either, just that the girl had been caught in the maze at Vauxhall Gardens with Lord Stapelton and was now forced to wed him though it was believed she harbored a tendre for his cousin instead.

Cameron straightened in his chair as his good friend, Lord Jeffries walked into the room. He cast a smile his way as he came and joined him at his table. "I didn't realize you were already in Town."

"I could say the same for you," Cameron retorted. "How rude of you not to send me a missive warning me of your impending arrival."

Lord Jeffries smiled at his teasing. "Now why would I want to do that? So you would have sufficient warning and have time to steal the hearts of the most beautiful ladies of the season before I got my chance at them? I would be a fool to allow that to happen."

Lord Jeffries signaled a server to bring him a drink.

"Speaking of beautiful ladies," Cameron said as he leaned over the table, "who should I be aware of?"

"If you mean to ask who I have set my cap for, you can forget it. Every time I express interest in a chit, you somehow manage to make them fall in love with you instead. I'd be a deuced fool to let that happen again."

"You're exaggerating, my friend. That only happened once, and if you remember correctly, I never returned the lady's devotion, and she quickly moved on to someone else."

"Someone else," he pointed out irritably, "that was not me."

Cameron laughed. "That was ages ago. I thought you forgave me when you realized how cow-handed she was."

"Clumsy or not, she was quite beautiful."

"And I can assure you there will be plenty of beautiful women for you to choose from this season as well. There always is. But who are you fooling? You aren't actually interested in the parson's mousetrap. If you were, you would have been wed ages ago."

"We aren't getting any younger," Lord Jeffries pointed out, his shoulders slumping in defeat. "Besides, my brother and his wife have yet to produce an heir, and my father has pointedly reminded me that if they fail to do so, the responsibility falls to me. Nothing like a little pressure to make me reconsider my bachelorhood."

Cameron cringed, feeling a measure of sympathy for his friend. Thankfully, his older brother had successfully produced an heir and a spare during his marriage, leaving Cameron free to do as he wished without any pressure to ensure the family line continues.

"Let us not speak of such...Thunder an' Turf," Lord Jeffries exclaimed, his eyes widening as he glanced over Cameron's shoulder.

"What is it, man?" Cameron's head turned, but he didn't see anything noteworthy behind him.

Lord Jeffries flapped his hand, drawing Cameron's attention back to him. "I just realized the time. I nearly forgot that I am expected at

Lord Straton's house for dinner tonight. My mother will have my head if I am late."

Lord Jeffries mother had recently wed Lady Straton's father, so the invitation to dine with them wasn't altogether surprising. What was surprising, however, was what his friend revealed next. "Lord Straton's sister is in town and has seemingly decided to participate in the season after living in hiding for the last four years since her husband's death. I suspect my mother has a bit of matchmaking up her sleeves, but I can assure you, I will not be party to it."

Cameron's ears perked up. "Why not? Is she whey-faced?"

He shrugged. "How am I to know? I've never met her. But my suspicions tell me she must be if she felt the need to hide from society for four years."

"Who was her late husband? Perhaps I know of the girl."

"The Baron Moncreif, nasty fellow from what I hear."

Cameron wanted to smile, but refrained. "Unfortunately, I don't know the girl. Best of luck to you tonight."

"Thanks," he grumbled, "I will need it."

Cameron watched patiently as his friend exited the club. As soon as he disappeared, he allowed a slow, satisfied smile to spread over his face. Lord Jeffries had been an unexpected source of information, but now he would be able to use his friend to aid him in his endeavors. What a lucky coincidence indeed.

Chapter Three

Rose tugged nervously at the low neckline of her gown, not liking the way it exposed more of her creamy bosom than she had ever bared. She blushed at the thought of Griffin seeing her in something so revealing.

"Stop that," Adel said as she swatted her hands away. "You look simply stunning."

Rose glanced once more at her reflection in the looking glass, not quite recognizing the woman who stared back at her. Her shiny raven locks had been pinned into a Grecian knot with several ringlets framing her face and the nape of her neck. Adel had pinched her cheeks so hard they were now contrasted a deep red against her alabaster skin. Taking a fortifying breath, she willed herself to look down at the rest of her body; a body hugged tightly in sapphire silk.

"I'm not quite sure I'm comfortable in this gown. I think the color is too bold."

Adel gasped. "The color is perfect. It sets off your pale skin and dark hair perfectly."

Rose turned, refusing to look at her reflection a moment longer. "But it's my first real season. I should be dressed in white and pastels."

"If you were a debutante, I would most certainly agree with that, but you are a widow, Rose. You have the freedom to wear things that a young girl just out of the school room does not. Besides, I do not want you to blend in with all of them. I want you standing out."

Rose groaned. "I do not mind blending in. Besides, Griffin will not be amused by this," she said, indicating her exposed neckline with the flick of one gloved hand.

One of Adel's eyebrows raised as she gave a coy grin, "Perhaps not, but certainly Lord Jeffries will be."

Rose's eyes widened as her mouth formed an o. "You are incorrigible."

Adel laughed as she grabbed Rose's arm and pulled her towards the door. "Let us be on our way; our company should arrive any moment."

By the time they arrived at the drawing room, Adel's father and his new wife were already present. Rose greeted the Earl and Countess cheerfully, though the entire time she wished to run back to her room to get a shawl.

"I must apologize for my son's late arrival," the countess interjected kindly once everyone, including Griffin, were present. "I'm afraid it's a common thing with Randolph."

Adel, ever the gracious host, merely smiled and assured her it was quite alright.

A quarter of an hour passed before Lord Jeffries finally arrived. Rose watched with amusement as the stocky man hurried into the drawing room, pulling nervously at his cravat. His eyes flashed towards his mother's as if he were waiting for her to scold him. Rose wanted to laugh.

"Randolph, how rude of you to keep us all waiting." she reprimanded. "Now do come here and allow me to introduce you to Lord Straton's sister, Lady Rose."

A small smile danced across her face as she waited for Lord Jeffries to approach. He wasn't precisely ugly, but she didn't find him overly handsome either. Instead, he reminded her of a big child, and she found her nerves suddenly calming in his presence. That is until his eyes dipped to her décolletage and widened with obvious delight. It was all Rose could do to allow him to take her hand and bow over it. She wanted to pull from his grasp and run to her room and change.

"My lady, I must confess that I am not entirely sorry for keeping you waiting."

"You're not?" she asked, confused.

"I find that you were worth the wait."

Rose took her hand back as her eyebrows scrunched together in confusion. Wasn't it them who had waited for him, not the other way around?

On the way to the dining room, Rose quickly pulled Adel aside and whispered, "I find I am quite chilled. I am going to go fetch a shawl and will meet you in the dining room at once."

"Very well, dearest, but please do hurry."

Rose nodded before heading off to her bedchamber. As soon as she entered, Prince streaked towards her, nearly knocking her to the ground. She laughed as she bent to stroke his soft, fluffy fur. "I wish I could take you to dinner, for I am certain I'd prefer your company to Lord Jeffries."

Prince barked in response. Rose patted him one last time before rushing to her closet to find a shawl. She chose a nice black one and quickly wrapped it around her shoulders, grateful for the covering it provided.

"Be a good boy, Prince, and I promise I will try to sneak you up a roll from dinner," she said as she patted his head and left.

Rose hurried down the stairs, not wanting her absence to give anyone reason to worry. She was almost to the landing when she heard the clattering of Prince's paws against the stairs behind her. Halting, she turned to watch as he bounced excitedly towards her.

"Drat, I must not have shut the door tightly," she scowled as she waited for him to approach.

With a measure of surprise, she watched as he barreled past her and began racing down the hall towards the foyer. She wanted to curse at the stupid dog, but instead she called after him, "Prince, get back here."

As per usual, he ignored her commands and kept running. Using one hand to hold tightly to her shawl, she used her other hand to lift her skirt so she could run after the big oaf. The butler was not particularly fond of Prince, and upon learning he was to reside with them for the season, he had made it clear that he expected the dog to keep his distance.

She picked up her pace as Prince got closer and closer to where the butler was standing, keeping his post by the door. "Get back here this instant, Prince," she shouted, upset that he kept ignoring her.

She felt several pins slip from her hair as she ran, but there was nothing to be done about it. She knew she was making a scene, but the only thing she cared about at that moment was keeping Prince away from the butler, for his frosty disdain was more than she could bear.

Just then, she felt her slipper catch on the hem of her gown. Her foot crashed down tugging on her dress and pulling her to a forceful halt. The problem was, her feet stopped but her body's momentum did not. Before she knew it, she was tumbling forward, the parquet floor coming up to meet her as she threw her hands out in front of her in an attempt to catch her fall.

***

Cameron and the butler grimaced in unison as the lady fell in a crumpled heap upon the ground. The butler had just opened the door at the precise moment she fell, giving him full access to the humiliating show. Before he could step into the foyer and offer her some assistance, a big, black cloud of fur came barreling towards him. He took a step back onto the porch and almost stumbled himself as the dog jumped up and began licking his face.

"Get down, you foul beast," the butler said as he displayed an extraordinary amount of strength and pulled the dog off of Cameron.

Cameron straightened his jacket and turned his attention once more to the lady. She had rolled on her back with her shawl splayed across the floor beneath her. His mouth went dry as his eyes settled on a deliciously indecent amount of exposed skin. It took him several seconds of staring before he realized the lady could be hurt and the gentlemanly thing to do would be to assist her instead of ogling her.

Rushing past the butler who was struggling to hold the dog in place, he went straight to the lady's side. Kneeling beside her he asked, "Are you alright?"

Her eyes were closed, and the only response he got was a groan.

His eyes quickly scanned her body for any injury, though it was hard to tell with her dress billowing out around her. He placed one hand on her cheek and leaned close. The scent of jasmine assaulted his senses. He was suddenly speechless as he stared at her pale face, her lashes dark and thick against her cheeks. His eyes dropped to her red lips, and he felt an overwhelming urge to bend down and kiss them.

Startled by his odd reaction, he stiffened as his eyes went to the butler. "Do something about that beast and come help me with the lady. She could be hurt."

It took some work, but the butler finally maneuvered the dog into the drawing room and quickly slammed the door shut, muttering curses underneath his breath as he made his way to Cameron's side. Cameron sprung into action. Lifting the lady into his arms, he turned to the butler and growled, "Where can I take her?"

The butler looked anxiously to the drawing room that now housed the dog. Cameron rolled his eyes. "Fiend seize it, show me to her bedchamber."

After a slight pause, the man did just that. Cameron had no problem carrying the girl up the two flights of stairs to her bedchamber;she wasn't very large. He wondered for a moment if she were Lady Moncreif, and if she were, how someone so small could be capable of murder.

Entering her bedchamber, Cameron took her straight to the bed where he laid her gingerly atop the mattress. Straightening, he turned to the butler and issued another order. "Go fetch someone who can assist her. I'm uncertain to what extent she may be injured."

The minute the butler left the room, the lady bolted up in the bed and groaned. Cameron spun around and gasped as her dark eyes glanced heavenward while she shook her head, looking completely miserable. He had most certainly met this lady before, for he knew he'd recognize those dark eyes anywhere. Rushing to her side, he observed her through squinted eyes. How did he know her?

"Lay down," he ordered. "You just had a bad fall and could be hurt."

"The only thing that is hurt," she seethed, her gaze locking with his, "Is my pride. Please leave at once and forget that you ever witnessed my folly." She slumped back into the mattress before turning on her side, away from him.

Cameron turned at the sound of rushing footsteps behind him. A man and a woman rushed into the room. The woman went instantly to the bed and reached for the lady now curled into a ball. "Rose, are you hurt?"

Rose? So, this was indeed Lady Moncreif, he thought with a hint of satisfaction.

Everyone in the room paused, waiting to hear the lady's response. "I'm fine," she mumbled, much to Cameron's relief. He was certain that more than anything, she was just painfully embarrassed.

"I'm sorry," the man said as he came to stand right next to Cameron. "I did not realize we were expecting any more company."

Cameron offered the man his hand, which he quickly took in a firm handshake. "You weren't," he responded. "I actually came to deliver this to Lord Jeffries." Cameron fumbled in his pocket until he found the pocket watch he had discreetly removed from Randolph's fob pocket while at White's. Extending it to the man at his side, he gave a self-deprecating laugh. "He mistakenly left it behind at White's. I raced here at once to ensure its safe return. I know how much it means to him and could not bear the thought of him fretting about its absence."

Cameron smiled shyly at the man as he slid the pocket watch into his large hand, then laughed nervously. He liked to pretend to be someone he was not. It made his job as an agent that much more amusing. He found that no one ever suspected the somewhat naive man of being anything other than what he portrayed.

"I will see that he gets it. But, I insist you join us for dinner. It's the least we can do to thank you for helping Rose."

Cameron glanced towards the bed where Lady Rose was now looking at him, waiting to hear his response. "I would be delighted," he said with a grin. He had not imagined the evening going so well and was quite pleased with this turn of events.

Chapter Four

It felt like hours had passed by before everyone left her bedchamber, though Rose knew it was only a matter of minutes. As soon as she heard the door shut, she heaved a loud sigh. Why had that man appeared in her life once more, and why at the most embarrassing of moments? She had dreamed of him countless times, but she had never had even a flicker of hope that those dreams would come true, that she would see him in the flesh once more. Perhaps that's why she allowed herself to think of him so often over the years —it was safe.

Straightening her bodice, she glanced down and noticed a tear in her skirt. She should have been mad that her new gown was ruined, but instead, she was pleased. Now she would have a perfectly good excuse to change, and this time she'd chose her own dress.

Clad in a simple, and high-necked gown of dark Primrose, Rose made her way carefully down the stairs. Her moves were slow and deliberate and a bit hesitant. She did not want to risk making a cake of herself once more.

All men stood as she entered the dining room. She inwardly groaned as she was shown to a seat between Lord Jeffries and Lord deCourtenay. She was pleased that the conversation all around the table resumed at once and everyone forgot about her. Her plate was filled with all sorts of delicious food, but all she could manage to do was scoot it around on her plate.

"Now I know how you stay so thin, Lady Rose," Lord Jeffries said by way of observation as he leaned back in his chair and patted his own stomach. "You have hardly eaten a thing."

Rose bristled at his comment but tried not to let her irritation show. There was no way he could know that she had actually gained some much-needed weight since her husband's death.

"In my humble opinion," Lord deCourtenay interjected, "I think she looks rather perfect." Then, turning his eyes on her, he added, "Ignore Randolph, he doesn't know what he's talking about."

In an attempt to ignore the way her whole body heated at his words, Rose quipped, "It's rather impolite of the both of you to speak of such things."

Lord Jeffries had the gumption to look contrite while Lord deCourtenay gazed at her thoughtfully for several long seconds before shrugging his broad shoulders and saying, "I suppose," then resumed eating his dinner.

Rose looked at him, her mouth agape. Was he truly so oblivious to his poor manners? In her state of irritation, she decided it was the perfect time to bring up another thing that was bothering her. Lowering her head close to Lord deCourtenay's, she hissed, "I want you to know that what happened tonight was all your fault."

"My fault?" he asked with dismay as he calmly lowered his fork to his plate.

"Yes. If you hadn't abandoned your dog and left him with me, this never would have happened."

A loud guffaw escaped from his mouth, causing several heads to turn. "So, you do recognize me."

Ignoring his question, she continued, "And if you have come to take Prince back, I will let you know right now that it will never happen. You told me I could have him and he is mine now."

"Thunder an' Turf, tell me you didn't name that poor animal after Prinny."

"The Prince Regent? No, of course not."

"What kind of a name is Prince anyway?"

"A perfectly good one," she shot back angrily.

"Perhaps if he were well mannered and charming, but he is anything but. Just look at what he did to you in the hall."

Rose stammered as she tried to make excuses for Prince. "How dare you judge him when you haven't even been around him the last four years. He's actually quite lovable and extraordinarily more adept at making conversation than you are."

Lord deCourtenay snorted as an amused grin spread across his face, revealing wickedly delicious dimples on both sides. "You mean to tell me that the dog actually talks? Blast it all, why did I ever give up such an extraordinary creature?"

Folding her arms across her chest, Rose huffed. "Of course he doesn't talk. That's what makes it all the more phenomenal. Without even saying a word he manages to surpass *you* in charm."

Leaning forward, Lord deCourtenay stared long and hard into her eyes. "I guess I will have to try harder to show you how incorrect you are, my dear. Charm is one thing I don't lack."

Apparently, Lord Jeffries had noticed Lord deCourtenay monopolizing her time, for just then he cut in. "Lady Rose, may I be so bold to ask, why of a sudden you have decided to participate in the season?"

Rose purposely squared her shoulders and turned away from Lord deCourtenay, giving Lord Jeffries all of her attention. "I thought, perhaps, that it might prove entertaining. I was getting quite bored with the current state of my life."

"Being a lonely widow?"

"More or less."

Lord deCourtenay leaned in, "Or perhaps you ran out of ways to...mourn your husband in the country and came to Town to find more creative ways to...deal with his death."

Everything inside of her bristled at his words. She felt her spine stiffen as she clamped her teeth down on the fleshy inside of her cheek. "What are you implying?"

He placed his napkin next to his plate and looked at her without the least bit of remorse. If he were implying that she was some sort of loose woman looking for a diversion, she would slap him. He had no idea the kind of woman she was, no idea at all.

"I wasn't implying anything about your character, my lady, but perhaps your guilt gives you away. What is the real reason you came to Town this season?"

Rising swiftly, Rose threw him a withering glare before turning and fleeing the dining room without another word. All eyes watched in shock as she left, a frosty silence filling the room. As soon as she disappeared from view, Rose let out a strangled sob. How dare Lord deCourtenay interrogate her as if she were some sort of wanton? She had dreamed about encountering him again, but tonight had been nothing but a nightmare.

She had reached the second flight of stairs when she heard a voice behind her. "Rose, wait." Ignoring Adel, she picked up her pace, for she was in no mood to talk to anyone.

By the time she reached her bedchamber, Adel had caught up to her. "Whatever happened back there?"

Rose's breathing was labored. "I don't wish to talk about it."

"But you must. If Lord Jeffries or Lord deCourtenay said something to offend you, I swear I will—"

"Expose them in your gossip column?" she asked, referring to a time long ago when Adel wrote a gossip column under the alias Mrs. Tiddlyswan.

Adel laughed. "Oh, what an excellent idea. Perhaps I shall start writing again, that way I can get even with anyone who displeases you."

Rose shook her head. "No, I insist you don't. I need to learn to handle life without you coming to my aide. Perhaps I was just being sensitive tonight. My dealings with the opposite sex have been severely limited."

Opening the bedchamber door, Adel ushered her inside. "Do not be so hard on yourself, for even women who have not been scarred like you have an awkward time dealing with men."

Rose looked at her sister-in-law skeptically. "I cannot imagine you ever having that problem."

"Oh, but I did. When I first met Griffin, I found him to be positively arrogant. We couldn't be around one another without quarreling. He was so overbearing, feeling as if he needed to protect me."

"From what?"

"From a marriage like yours. He knew that my mother had just died and was worried my father would do the same thing yours did—marry me off to the first man who offered. Watching you suffer was not easy on him."

"I know, but somehow everyone managed to move on. Everyone but me, that is."

Adel wrapped her arms around Rose. "You will never fully move on. Your past has created your present. You are who you are because of what you've been through."

"A pathetic woman who acts more like a scared little child?"

"No," Adel exclaimed with exasperation. "You are much, much

more than that. We all have personal demons, Rose, but if we chose to let those define us instead of looking for and magnifying our strengths, we would be most miserable indeed."

Later that night as Rose lay in the dark stillness of her bedchamber, she thought back to Adel's words. Being miserable was something she knew an awful lot about, and quite frankly, she was growing tired of it. With renewed determination, she decided she would try harder not to let her emotions get the best of her so that she could learn to find joy in life without letting her past define her.

Chapter Five

His eyes roamed over the list several times, but his head could not seem to process the information he was reading. Cameron was too busy worrying about the poor impression he had made on Lady Rose and fretting over how he would make it up to her to pay attention to the list before him. He had been foolish to be so bold on their first encounter, interrogating her and treating her with suspicion. Of course, that's what he was supposed to be doing, but he was supposed to be much more discreet about it. She should never have had any inkling that he was prodding her for information.

When questioned about her abrupt disappearance at dinner, he was able to feign ignorance, though he apologized profusely for anything he may have said or done to upset her. Thankfully Lord Straton saw nothing more than a confused man who was completely innocent of any wrongdoing. Had her brother had so much as a hint that he had offended his sister, he was certain the man would never let him around her again, and that would just not do. He was grateful his acting skills had worked better on Lady Rose's brother than they seemed to on her.

A long, heavy sigh escaped his lips as he shook his head in frustration. What was it about the girl that made him forget himself and every notable skill he had developed in his years as an agent? Of course, she was beautiful, especially since her angular face and too thin frame had filled out in the years since their first encounter, but she was not any more attractive than all the other women of the *ton*.

As his eyes returned once more to the list in front of him, a list containing all the names of persons who had won a significant amount of money from Lord Moncreif, he forced himself to focus on the task at hand, reminding himself that Lady Rose could very well be a killer. Any one of these men could be in danger of losing their life if he didn't find out who the murderer was and put a stop to it. The weight of his assignment weighed heavily upon him.

Thinking once more of Lady Rose, he wondered if she could truly be capable of such crimes. It's true that she was not very large in stature, but administering poison to a person did not require any particular amount of strength. Her physical abilities were far inferior to what she was mentally capable of plotting and executing.

Lady Rose might be slight, but she was fierce. Of course, she did not come across that way in the least, certainly not upon the first encounter, and definitely not to most people, but the other night at dinner he had seen something in her that he guessed rarely came to the surface. Suppressed anger was brewing just below the surface, waiting to boil over and scorch anyone it touched. He could tell by the rude comments he had made to provoke her that she didn't particularly like men, especially him, and he vowed to find out why.

But of course, he knew that he needed to take a different tactic if he ever hoped to win her esteem and gain access to her hidden persona. He needed to charm her, to make her trust him implicitly, a feat that shouldn't be too hard seeing as how he was well versed in wooing the ladies. The grin returned to his face. Yes, the only way he would get anywhere with Lady Rose was by showing her just how charming he could be and he was perfectly certain he would have no problems doing just that.

Cameron was feeling particularly confident by the time the Jeffersen ball rolled around that night. Dressed in the height of fashion and determined to win Lady Rose's esteem, his eyes scoured the dance floor until they rested upon her, dancing with Lord Summers. He studied her face from across the room, noting the stiff smile and rapidly blinking eyes. She was not at all comfortable with the man. Pride welled up inside of him as he waited patiently for the dance to end, for he knew that once he claimed her, her discomfort would evaporate.

He wasn't the least bit surprised when she greeted him with clipped tones when he approached to ask for a dance. He saw the hesitation in her eyes and at once flashed her one of his most charming smiles. "I promise I will behave myself tonight. I'm feeling quite contrite about the way things were left with us before and had only hoped you would allow me the chance to apologize."

After a brief pause, she reluctantly took his arm and allowed him to lead her to the floor. Cameron placed his hand on her back and pulled her close. The waltz began, and though he noted she was not the most graceful of dancers, he liked the way she felt in his arms.

Smiling down upon her he said, "His name was Roland."

She looked at him confused. "Whose name, my lord?"

"Your dog's," he stated slowly, placing emphasis on the fact that Prince was now hers.

"What a horrendous name."

"That name belonged to my father's favorite hunting dog; I'll have you know. I find it perfectly respectable, more decent than Prince if you ask me."

"Well, I don't. And I didn't mean to insult your father; I only meant that Roland does not suit my Prince at all." She shuddered in his arms.

"Can I ask you why you find Prince to be such an exceptional name for the beast?

He watched with amusement as she blushed, and not just slightly. Her alabaster skin flushed a deep red as her eyes instantly dropped from his face. She even stumbled upon his feet. He hadn't realized his question would be so upsetting, but her reaction made him all the more curious.

"Please tell me why you selected such a name, for you're making me increasingly curious."

"I can't," she muttered, still avoiding eye contact.

"Then perhaps I shall take a guess. Hmmm," he said thoughtfully, very much enjoying her discomfort. "Could it be that you named him after your dearly departed prince?"

Her eyes snapped up to his, confusion marring her brow. "My prince?"

"Your husband," he explained.

Cameron was baffled when every muscle in the lady's body tensed. Instead of feeling soft and pliable in his arms, she felt stiff. He suddenly felt as if he were dancing with a board, one that was casting the most hateful of glances at him.

"Whoa," he exclaimed, as he willed her to loosen up a bit by rubbing small circles on her back. "I can see that I said the wrong thing once more. I have a penchant for offending you, my lady, and I swear that is not my intent."

"Then what is your intent?"

He searched her eyes, knowing full well he couldn't tell her the truth. It was true that the dark pools were flashing angrily at him, but the longer he stared at them, the more he noticed that the anger was simply masking something else. Deep within the hidden recesses was a pain unlike any he had seen before. Her face was haunted, her soul was sad, he could sense that much in one single glance. The realization sent him reeling.

His voice was husky with emotion when he finally admitted, "I simply want to be your friend." He knew it didn't answer her question and he knew it wasn't the full intent of his mission, but at that moment he realized it was the truest thing he had yet to say to her.

"My friend?" she stuttered in disbelief.

"Yes. Is that so hard to believe?"

"I don't have many friends," she admitted honestly, her emotions surprisingly raw.

"Well," he said with a grin, "you are now one friend richer."

Cameron had hoped to get a smile in return, but Lady Rose did nothing but nod slowly. At least she hadn't refused his offer, for he wasn't sure how his pride would handle such a blow. Feeling like he had made some headway in winning her favor, he led her back to Lady Straton's side as soon as the dance ended. He was surprised at the plethora of feelings that assaulted him as he left her. Part of him wanted to run as fast and as far away from the vulnerable little creature, while another part of him wanted to scoop her into his arms and kiss her so soundly that she forgot whatever reason she had to be sad.

He quickened his pace and moved to the opposite side of the room, putting as much distance between them as he could. He grabbed a glass of champagne off a passing tray and began drinking it. He needed to clear his mind. Forcing the odd interaction out of his head, he reminded himself that Lady Rose was suspected of committing many murders and that he was not sent by the Main Office to befriend the suspect but to prove her guilty. Or innocent, he reasoned, trying to remain impartial, of course.

He began pacing the perimeter of the ballroom, his eyes roaming the crowds for any of the people on the list he had been memorizing earlier that day. He noticed Lord Beauchamp in the corner speaking animatedly to several young debutantes, clearly enjoying the attention he was receiving. He glanced surreptitiously to Lady Rose to see if she was aware of him. He gasped sharply when he noticed her being led onto the dance floor by Mr. Fox, another man who had been on the list.

He made his way to a corner and half hid behind a large plant as he shrewdly watched the pair. Lady Rose kept laughing at something Mr. Fox was saying and quite frankly; it bothered Cameron. Mr. Fox had a reputation for being quite forward with women and the thought that he was flirting with Lady Rose and that she was enjoying it bothered him. Did he not realize he was flirting with danger? Of course, he didn't he grumbled beneath his breath, but his irritation remained nonetheless.

As soon as the dance ended, Cameron watched Mr. Fox lead Lady Rose through the French doors out into the gardens. He instantly straightened before disappearing from the room. He had to get to the gardens and spy on the couple. The fact that Lady Rose could be doing something dangerous propelled him forward. He couldn't, in good conscience, allow Mr. Fox to be alone with the suspected killer. At least, that's what he kept telling himself as he made his way quietly from the house, slipping around to the gardens, making sure he kept in the shadows so he wouldn't be noticed.

Truth be told, the real fear he harbored was that Mr. Fox would do something indecent to Lady Rose. If that man so much as made an attempt at compromising her, he would call him out. He hid within a copse of trees, confident that no one could see him as his eyes followed the couple on their stroll.

He felt confused as he warred with the emotions battling within him. Not one assignment had ever caused him to feel so conflicted. All the evidence gathered pointed to Lady Rose as the culprit, yet here he was, standing in the shadows of the trees, feeling more need to protect her than her potential victim. What was wrong with him?

The couple sat on a bench and continued their conversation. Oh, how he wished he hadn't been so impulsive in following them out. Standing in the shadows, too far away to hear the conversation between the pair, he wished he had had the foresight to bring a lady on a stroll so he wouldn't be confined to his hiding place.

Cameron would have kicked himself if he could. He had made too many errors tonight to count, and it frustrated him endlessly. He stayed in the trees until Mr. Fox escorted Lady Rose back inside, feeling like a fool for spying on her when he had been unable to garner any information. At least he felt a sense of relief that Mr. Fox had not attempted anything indecent towards the lady.

As soon as he returned to the ballroom, Lord Jeffries joined him at his side. "You have eyes for her, don't you?"

Cameron peeled his eyes from Lady Rose to glance at his friend. "For who?"

Lord Jeffries stared at him as if he were a fool. "Lady Rose, of course. I saw the way you flirted with her at dinner, and I see the way you can't keep your eyes off of her tonight. Thunder an' Turf, I'm glad I wasn't interested in the chit, for I'd hate to have my heart broken by you once more."

Rolling his eyes, he walked towards the edge of the room. "Do not speak so foolishly. I did not flirt with Lady Rose, and I most certainly am not interested in her." Then, to attempt to prove his point, he lied to his friend. "I think you and Lady Rose would make a most excellent match. It would be worth your time to pursue her and see where it leads."

"You really think so?" he asked, his eyes sparkling with glee. "I admit that I do find her appearance quite pleasant to behold. Her pixie-like features are most charming. And, I rather liked the way she didn't pander to your wishes as most ladies are want to do."

"I didn't make any requests of her," Cameron growled, his hackles raised by his friend's innocent words.

Lord Jeffries laughed. "No, but she certainly wasn't smitten with you, which came as a great relief to me. By Zeus, perhaps I am more enamored with the girl than I had supposed. Perhaps I will excuse myself and go ask for a dance. I'd love to see how she fits in my arms."

"You go do that," Cameron muttered crossly as Lord Jeffries walked away, his step light with anticipation.

Cameron watched long enough to see Lord Jeffries eagerly take Lady Rose in his arms before he turned away and cursed underneath his breath. Tonight had been beyond frustrating and unproductive. There was no need for him to stay around and watch Lord Jeffries woo Lady Rose. Turning on his heel, he exited the ball, relieved that he would no longer have to watch her flit about in other men's arms.

Chapter Six

Fueled on by a sense of concern for the gentleman of the *ton* whose lives were in danger, Cameron left the ball and headed straight for Lord Straton's townhouse. He had to do some investigating, and he knew now would be the perfect time to do it while the entire family was occupied and absent.

He instructed his driver to park the carriage several streets away, then told him to wait while he disappeared into the night. Fortunately, his staff could be trusted and never questioned him when asked to do something absurd.

The streets were empty and the night air was brisk. Cameron hurried along until he approached the townhouse, sliding along the edge until he found himself standing at the back of the house, inspecting each window hoping to find one that would be easy to jar open. His long fingers slid beneath a window that had been left partially ajar then he slid it slowly open, careful not to make a peep.

He held his breath and waited for several long seconds to see if any servants were about. Confident that they weren't, he stuck his head inside and tuned his ears to hear the noises of the house. His eyes adjusted to the darkness and he realized the window led into the breakfast room. He could hear the muted ticking of a clock that was somewhere in the room, but other than that, the house was silent.

He crawled through the open window and straightened as he entered the house. Turning, he slid the window shut, careful to leave it open a crack, just as it had been before. He tiptoed across the wood floor, stealthy as a cat. He had much practice with entering places in such a manner. It was all a part of his job.

Though he knew nothing about the layout of this particular townhouse, he knew that he could find Lady Rose's bedchamber on the second floor. All the London townhouses had that much in common, in his experience. His step was light as he made his way quickly and quietly to the staircase and up to the second floor. He began opening doors one at a time until he found the bedchamber he strongly suspected was hers. It was feminine yet simple, much like her. And the biggest giveaway of all was the fact that Prince was lying perfectly still in the middle of the bed.

Fiend seize it, he had not taken that complication into account when he had decided to come tonight. He stood completely still against the now closed door and waited to see if the dog would sense his presence. He would have to be extremely careful if he wished to accomplish his purposes without disturbing the beast.

He pulled at his cravat to loosen it, suddenly feeling warm. Creeping forward, he made his way to the large closet that housed Lady Rose's wardrobe. His fingers slid over gowns of fine silk as he inspected the entire contents of the closest hoping to find some piece of incriminating evidence.   Dropping to his knees, he began inspecting each and every tiny slipper, turning them over and shaking them out in the hopes that perhaps a pouch of poison would be hiding inside. He realized that his actions seemed absurd, but knew from experience how effective they could be. He had found more than one piece of evidence in this manner in the past and was hopeful that tonight's search would prove just as fruitful. Convinced that there was nothing noteworthy in the closet, he rose from the floor. He would need to make his way into the bedchamber now and continue his search without waking up Prince.

He bent down and removed his shoes, knowing his stocking feet would make less noise, and left them in the closet as he made his way into the bedchamber. A quick search of her jewelry box and desk produced nothing extraordinary. He wasted no time moving on to the dresser against the wall. His neck felt warm as he opened one drawer to reveal several articles of underclothing. He gingerly picked up a chemise and willed himself not to think of Lady Rose wearing nothing but the thin article.

He quickly refolded the item and placed it back in the stack exactly as he had found it, feeling awkward about the fact that he was rummaging through her most personal of belongings. He knew without a doubt that she would be mortified if she knew he had handled such things.

Good thing she'll never find out, he thought as he moved on to the remaining two drawers in the dresser. Disappointingly, they too held nothing but clothing articles as well. He turned around and scanned the room for anything he may have missed when his eyes settled upon the trunk at the foot of the bed. He hurried to the trunk and knelt before it as he quickly pried it open. The lid gave an ear-splitting creak, and his heart began beating wildly in his chest. The noise seemed to echo loudly throughout the room.

In the middle of the bed, Prince began to toss. Cameron glanced from the trunk back to the closet, wondering if he should make a dash for it. His hands were frozen to the lid of the trunk as he waited to see what he should do. He wanted to curse as the dog awoke, his ears perking straight up as his eyes settled directly on Cameron and he began to bark.

Cameron bolted to his feet. "Hush, you mutt," he hissed, praying the dog would stop barking. He rushed to Prince's side and stuck out his hand for him to sniff. "It's me, your former owner. I'm not here to hurt you." When the dog stopped barking, he instantly rewarded him by petting his thick mane of fur. Prince nuzzled into his palm, soaking up every bit of attention.

He looked heavenward and muttered a thank you before returning to the trunk and deftly inspecting the contents inside, his new best friend not leaving his side for even one minute. He momentarily forgot the purpose of his search as he became intrigued with what he was discovering inside. The trunk was filled with several articles of baby clothing, covered in intricate embroidery. He didn't have an eye for such things, but even he could tell that they were exceptional works of quality. He wondered if they were the product of Lady Rose or of someone else, and why she would feel the need to keep such things.

In a corner at the bottom of the trunk, he found a stack of letters tied together with a hair ribbon. Curious, he removed them and made his way to the window where the bright moon was letting in a fair amount of light. He untied the ribbon and laid it aside as he began unfolding the worn parchment and reading the contents of the letters as he leaned against the window sill.

The first letter was addressed to Lord Westingham whom he recognized at once as her father from the information he had gathered on her.

> *I have had ample time to consider how to best broach this subject with you, but I have yet to get the courage to actually send this missive. Perhaps I may never do so, but I feel compelled to write it nonetheless.*

> *Why? That's the question that weighs so heavily upon me. I always tried to be a good daughter and never cause you any undue concern, yet you cast me aside as if I had been nothing but a troublesome burden to you.*

> *I am certain you know of my plight, and yet you do nothing to assist me. My heart breaks knowing that my own father has*

completely abandoned me and left me to this tragic fate. Have you no love left for me in your heart? Perhaps I don't want to know the answer to that.

Cameron's heart twisted in his chest as he read the sad words. He wasn't certain to what she was referring, but the pain in her penned words pierced him to his soul. In an attempt to ignore the pain he felt on the lady's behalf, he quickly unfolded the next missive.

Esther,

It's foolish of me to even pen this missive when I know that you will never read it. Even if I had a way of knowing where to send it, I am uncertain I would have the courage to do so.

I feel utterly, foolishly betrayed by your actions. Why did you turn against me? You were my only friend for years, yet it was you who divulged the information to my husband that put the life of another in danger.

I understand that you suffered unduly during our time together, but no more so than I. Your actions caused heartache and pain, and I cannot find a reason for them no matter how hard I have tried. Please, I plead with you, explain yourself. Give me some reason to hope that your intentions weren't evil and that it was simply a mistake.

Cameron read this particular missive over and over again, unsure of what to make of it. Who was Esther and what had she done to betray Lady Rose? He turned the parchment over hoping there would be a full name written on it somewhere, but there was no additional information to be found. With frustration, he folded the missive up and moved on to the final one. This missive was not addressed to anyone, but it was the most heart wrenching one yet.

I hate you from the very depths of my soul. I feel nothing but anger when I think of your name. Your sole purpose during our relationship was to use me as an object of your satisfaction, and use me you did. You hurt me in ways I can't make myself pen. To relive those moments, even just in written word, is to take me back to a time in my life I would give anything to erase. I wish you had never been born. I wish I had never laid eyes upon your evil face. And though I will never admit it to another living soul, I wish more than anything it had been me that shot you that fateful day.

Cameron was startled by a door banging shut. He stiffened as he tucked the letters into his pocket. The noise had come from the hall, but he suddenly feared that he would get caught. He ran across the room, Prince at his heels, and retrieved his shoes from the closet, sliding his feet into them as fast as he could. He didn't dare leave through the door for fear of being discovered. He raced to the window and looked out hoping there was some way he could escape safely but unfortunately, he could see no way of doing it without risking breaking his neck.

Footsteps sounded in the hall, and he panicked. Glancing around the room, he noticed Prince had finally left his side and was now waiting anxiously at the door for his mistress to return, his tail wagging wildly behind him. Cameron quickly did the only thing he could think to do, he slid underneath the bed and prayed that no one would discover him.

His heart was beating violently against his chest as the door creaked open slowly. He held his breath and watched two dainty slippers appear in the room as Prince nearly bombarded the girl as he eagerly greeted his mistress.

Rose laughed. "Oh, Prince, I missed you."

Prince barked in response.

"Shush," Lady Rose gently scolded. "You know that Griffin will throw you out on your ear if you wake one of the children. You must consider yourself lucky that he allows you in the house at all. You know how much he loathes you."

"Lady Rose?" a soft voice called out as someone else entered the room. "I came to ready you for bed."

Cameron was growing quite warm being trapped beneath the bed. At that moment, the only thing he could wonder was precisely how long it took a lady to ready for bed and fall asleep. He hoped it was quick. He closed his eyes and rested his forehead against the hard floor below. He was grateful, at least, that it wasn't covered in dust. The maids were clearly doing a fine job. He briefly wondered if underneath his own bed was as pristine.

A loud swoosh of fabric accompanied by a gust of air startled him from his pointless ruminations. He glanced to the side and noticed a dress piled haphazardly on the floor. The vision he beheld next made his mouth go dry. Stepping out of that pile of fabric was the most slender and shapely legs he had ever beheld. He was close enough to see that the skin was creamy white and looked incredibly soft. He had been mistaken earlier when he thought it hot beneath the bed. Now, it was downright blistering.

He itched to loosen his cravat but knew he couldn't risk so much movement. Instead, he stared helplessly as those divine legs walked across the room and disappeared into the closet. His mind flitted back to the chemise he'd held earlier and wicked visions involving Lady Rose at once overtook him. He wanted to groan in agony.

Loud sniffing sounds interrupted his fantasies. He hesitantly opened his eyes only to find himself face to face with Prince's snout. At that point, he was pretty certain he did groan out loud. The dratted beast sniffed at him as if he were a large slice of roast beef before he began licking him. Cameron held his breath, his cheeks puffing out as he tried not to reprimand the animal. He knew if he gave any response, it would only encourage Prince to continue. He hoped by remaining still the dog would stop sooner.

"What are you doing, Prince?" Lady Rose asked.

Cameron's heart stilled as he prayed harder than he ever remembered doing. How in the world would he explain his presence underneath the bed to Lady Rose, let alone to her brother?

He heard the lady shudder. "Please tell me there is not a mouse beneath my bed. I will never fall asleep if that is the case."

Did she truly expect the dog to answer her?

"Quit that nonsense at once, boy," she urged in a mildly authoritative voice, "and get up here with me."

He was totally and utterly surprised that the dog did as she commanded, at once withdrawing from him and jumping on the mattress. Perhaps that dog wasn't so foolish after all. Cameron was positive he would never have hesitated to crawl into bed with the lady had she ordered him to do so.

He was uncertain how much time passed as he anxiously waited for her to fall asleep. It intrigued him that she sang soft lullabies to Prince before eventually falling silent. He waited for a long time afterward until he felt positive that she was asleep before sliding from beneath the bed.

His body was stiff from staying in the same position for so long. He stretched his limbs out, feeling relieved to be able to move freely once more. He knew he needed to be on his way, but he took a moment to stare gently down upon Lady Rose who was curled up in a ball next to Prince. She looked so tiny next to the brute. His entire being ached to curl up beside her and protect her, for she looked so vulnerable laying in the large bed in nothing but her white cotton nightdress. Of course, he resisted the urge and forced himself to leave. He'd be lucky if his driver was still waiting for him.

Right before he reached the door he heard a small whimper behind him. He spun around and watched as Lady Rose turned on her side, her face marred with sadness though she remained fast asleep. He went to her side and allowed himself to reach forth and stroke her face ever so gently. Her skin was soft and delicate beneath his touch. His thumb brushed against the very corner of her mouth, and he recoiled at once, feeling as if his fingers had been singed.

He blinked several times in shock wondering what the strange reaction could mean before quickly retreating from the room. He had to get away from the confounded lady before he became her next victim.

Chapter Seven

Rose awoke suddenly from her dream. She blinked several times rapidly as she tried to convince herself it had meant nothing. In her dream, Lord deCourtenay had come to her and urged her to leave with him. At first, she had been confused by his pleading, wondering why she would leave with a man she hardly knew. Before she had a chance to voice her questions, however, he was reaching for her hands. She at once recoiled from his touch, hiding them in her skirts so he couldn't see the ugly scars that covered them, stretching up both arms like the twisted vines that grew up the side of her childhood home.

"Give them to me at once," he urged, his voice no longer pleading but commanding.

His insistence frightened her, and she took a hearty step backward at the same moment he lunged for her. Without thinking, she removed her hands from their hiding place and used them to shield her face instead.

A loud gasp echoed across the room, but she was too scared to look. "Who in tarnation did this to you?"

She felt herself begin to shake, but she willed herself not to respond to his question. With her eyes tightly closed, she began counting in her head, slowly, methodically, like she always did when she was about to be attacked.

She felt the first contact and flinched as his hands came to rest upon her shoulders. It took everything inside of her not to whimper. In so many ways the anticipation was worse than the actual beating itself.

Warm air fanned across her hands that were still covering her face. "Rose," he whispered, his voice filled with painful emotion. "I am not going to harm you."

She heard his words perfectly, but she couldn't seem to believe them.

"Rose," he whispered once more, "you must trust me. I'm here to protect you."

She gave a mirthless laugh. No one had ever been her protector before, why would that suddenly change? Without her permission, he reached forth and clasped her wrists and pulled her hands forcibly from her face. She tried to cry out, but no sound escaped her throat. She stared at his long fingers encircling her wrists in horror. What was he doing to her? Why wouldn't he let her go? She struggled against his grasp, but he was relentless in his hold.

"Rose," his voice was more urgent this time as his consuming gaze bore into her. "You must trust me. I can't protect you unless you do."

His muted green eyes were not striking in color, but it wasn't the color the drew her in, it was the intensity of his gaze. He stood staring into her soul, and she felt something thaw within her heart. Could she trust him? Would he really save her?

"Please," he urged huskily.

Tears started coursing down her cheeks as she warred within herself. How could she trust someone she didn't even know?

He surprised her by answering the question she hadn't spoken out loud. "You do know me. You always have. I'm the prince you dreamed up in your fantasies, the man who was created to save you. But I can't, not unless you let me."

She looked down at her hands then and realized he no longer had a hold of them. His own arms were outstretched, waiting for her to give herself to him in trust. She gazed long and hard upon her ugly, scarred hands. The lighting in the room was deplorable, making the normally reddish scars appear an angry purple. They hardly ever hurt anymore unless she bumped them against something. Then, the pain would become almost unbearable, the memories fresh.

Her eyes looked up and captured his once more while a seed of trust sprouted in her heart. She had two options—she could either keep the scars and the hidden pain for the rest of her life or trust that this man standing before her would save her. Her hands shook as she reached for his still outstretched ones. The minute his large hands enveloped hers, she quit shaking. Looking down and gasped, the scars on her hands were completely gone.

"How did you do it?" she asked breathily, unwilling to look away from her healed hands and arms.

"You did it," he replied, "by allowing yourself to trust."

That is when she had woken up. Without even thinking, she glanced to her arms, which looked as they always did—pale and unmarred. What did the odd dream mean and why did it feel so real? She curled on her side, snuggling into the still sleeping Prince hating the way sadness and regret and fear mixed in her stomach making her feel ill.

She rarely ever thought back to her own invisible scars that her husband had caused by his abuse, but the dream had left them ripped open and exposed. She knew that she was safe now and that Lord Moncreif would never harm her again, but some days the memories hurt nearly as bad as the beatings had.

Her spirit had nearly been killed during the two years she had been wed to the despicable baron, not to mention what he had done to her body. He had abused her in every way possible and since he had been her husband, it had been his right to do with her as he pleased. His death had been nothing short of a miracle, for it was the only way she could have ever been freed from his clutches.

Prince woke up then and at once began licking her face. She tried to smile at the dog, but couldn't even manage that much. Thoughts of her dead husband and the horrendous life she had led as his wife had given her the doldrums. Why did she have to be plagued with dreams such as the one she just awoke from? They did nothing but crush her spirits.

She refused to get out of bed but Prince, on the other hand, was more than ready to begin his day. He jumped off the bed and began prancing around the room. She was certain he needed to be let outside to relieve himself, but she couldn't seem to make herself get up to see to the task. She silently prayed that her maid would show up soon and do it for her.

When she could no longer hear the scratching of his paws against the wood floor, she panicked and shot from the bed. He better not be relieving himself in her bedchamber! She glanced to where he was huddled beneath her window, playing with something she couldn't quite see.

Forcing herself from the bed, she called out, "Come on, boy, let's take you out."

He stood up on all fours and lazily turned to look at her, a faded purple ribbon hanging from his mouth. Rose gasped, recognizing the ribbon at once. She ran fourth and grabbed it and began pulling. "Where did you get that from?"

Prince, unwilling to give up his treasure, pulled back and an impromptu game of tug-of-war ensued. When it became apparent that she was not going to win, she finally gave up. "Keep it then," she snapped angrily before making her way to the trunk at the foot of the bed. It wasn't the ribbon that was important to her anyway; it was the letters that she had tied up with it that mattered.

She threw the lid of the trunk open and began rummaging through the contents, throwing things about haphazardly as she prayed she would find the missives she had written in moments of anger and never sent. They were personal and private, and it mortified her to think that someone may have read them.

Alarm filled her breast when she realized they were missing. Who had been in her room and taken them? She instantly wondered if one of Griffin and Adel's boys had been playing in there and found them, the thought instantly filling her breast with worry. If it had been one of them, had they found the other thing she kept hidden as well?

Her hands shook violently as she searched through a small stack of books until she found the nondescript one with the brown faded binding. She quickly opened it to reveal a hidden compartment. She exhaled in relief when she saw the tarnished gold locket still sitting inside. With shaking fingers, she pulled the necklace from the opening and fingered it for a moment, letting the chain slither against her palm.

Lord Moncreif had given her the simple locket on their wedding day. He said that it had belonged to his first wife and that he had wanted her to have it. She remembered his pudgy hands struggling to clasp it into place around her neck before the wedding ceremony. It wasn't until their wedding night that he made her open it and see what was inside.

She was laying naked in his bed, shaking from the violent lovemaking he had just forced upon her. She didn't want to do as he bid but had recently learned that he did not take no for an answer. His evil gaze never left her as she struggled to open the clasp, her hands shaking like a leaf in the wind.

Her eyes registered confusion as a small satchel fell out and landed on the mattress next to her. She turned questioning eyes on her new husband.

"It's poison," he said calmly as if they were discussing something as mundane as crumpets and tea. "It's the only way you will ever escape me."

It took several seconds for his meaning to sink in. He was telling her that she would have to kill herself to get away from him. The nightmare had only just begun.

Shaking her head to dispel the atrocious memory, Rose used her fingernail to pry open the clasp. The satchel of poison was still inside. Relief flooded her entire being. Thank goodness one of her nephews hadn't found it. She should have gotten rid of it years ago, but she very seldom ever went through the contents of the trunk and had easily forgotten that the locket even existed.

Squishing the satchel back into the locket, she pressed it tightly shut and clasped it around her neck. Today would be the day she got rid of it once and for all.

Chapter Eight

Rose startled as her sister-in-law entered the room without warning. She quickly snapped her head towards the door where Adel was smiling vibrantly. Her auburn hair had already been done, and her lovely jonquil walking dress indicated she was ready for an outing.

"I came to ask you if you would like to go shopping on Bond Street."

Rose glanced down at the scattered items of the trunk. Ignoring Adel's question, she asked, "Did the children come in my bedchamber this morning?"

Adel gave her a curious look. "I do not believe so. They have been with their nanny all morning. Why do you ask?"

"Because I am missing something important from my trunk. I don't know who would have taken it."

"Oh no," Adel exclaimed. "What is missing?"

"Some letters. I had them bundled together and tied with a ribbon. Prince found the ribbon on the floor and was playing with it."

"Do you think your maid took them?"

"No."

"Perhaps Prince ate them," Adel suggested.

Both women turned and looked at the fluffy dog who was still finding amusement with said ribbon, completely unaware of their conversation.

"Perhaps he could have," Rose admitted, though that still didn't explain how he would have gotten them from her trunk.

"I'm sorry, Rose. Were they of great importance to you?"

Rose was thoughtful. The letters were not important, not really. She had written them more for her own healing than for anything else. She knew she would never dare send them, though she held onto them anyway in case she ever changed her mind and got the courage to do so. The thought of losing the letters didn't cause her much distress, what worried her so was that someone had been in her room, going through her most personal of belongings.

"Not really," she finally answered. "I suppose it's past time I got rid of some of this stuff anyway," she said, flinging her hand towards the belongings scattered about the floor.

Adel picked up a baby bonnet covered in the most intricate of stitches and held it to her chest. "But what if you need it someday?"

Tears welled up in her eyes, but Rose was quick to force them down. She looked at Adel sadly, her lower lip shaking with emotion. The woman meant well, but her high hopes and dreams for Rose seemed impossible.

"I'm uncertain I will ever wed. And," she forced herself to admit, "even if I did, I am not a fool to believe I'll ever be blessed with children."

Adel fell to her knees and scooped Rose into her arms. She stroked her long, black hair as hot tears scalded Rose's cheeks. "Oh my dearest, you do not know that you will never bear a child. You must remain hopeful."

Though her words were meant to soothe, they only caused more sorrow for Rose. She had been with child five times during her marriage to Lord Moncreif and not once was she able to carry a baby past a few months. She knew that was because of her husband's violent beatings, but in her heart, she wondered if her body had been damaged beyond repair.

"But who would even consider wedding a woman who might never be able to produce an heir?"

Adel pulled back and looked at her in shock. "Is that why you refuse to open your heart to fall in love? Because you fear that you are somehow not worthy?"

Rose searched her face, afraid to admit the true depths of her feelings.

"I truly loathe your late husband. He was a poor excuse of a man. Men marry women all of the time with no certainty that they'll be able to provide them with an heir."

"But they marry them with the hopes that they will. Lord Moncreif resented the fact that I couldn't produce an heir for him."

Adel's eyes flashed with anger. "Then he should have considered keeping his hands off of you. He was a murderer," she cried out in anger. Rose flinched at her strong words as Adel continued, "He killed your babies, Rose. I am certain he would have eventually killed you had he not killed himself first. I cannot bear the thought that he still wields any influence over you."

"He does not," she snapped defensively.

"Oh, but he does. He spent the entirety of your marriage killing your spirit while he took advantage of your body. Though he is no longer here to beat you, he is still somehow able to convince you that you have no value and that no one will ever want you. Don't you see that?" she pleaded emotionally.

Rose was thoughtful as her eyes slid to the floor. Adel was right. "I thought I had come a long way in letting it go. While living at the cottage, it was easy to forget about him. Perhaps that's because my life was so vastly different there than the life I lived with him. Being in London for the season has caused all sorts of strange emotions to resurface. Perhaps it was a poor idea for me to come."

"Nonsense," Adel exclaimed as she let go of Rose and began throwing the contents of the trunk back inside. "You simply need to give yourself permission to heal, and you will never do that while you are holding on to any piece of the past. I will instruct the servants to remove this trunk while we are gone. You will never have to see any reminder of your past life again."

Rose glanced carefully at the items Adel was throwing haphazardly into the trunk. Truthfully, there was nothing inside that didn't have some tie to her miserable marriage. Most of the items were articles of baby clothing she had embroidered and saved in hopes of using someday. But Adel was right, she had to get rid of all reminders of her past before she could begin looking fully to the future. With a renewed sense of hope, she began throwing the belongings in as well.

When everything was returned to the trunk and the lid had been shut tightly, Adel stood and helped Rose do so as well. "Now, I will send your maid in to get you ready, for an excursion to Bond Street will prove to be a most excellent distraction. Perhaps we can find you a new bonnet to cheer you."

Rose managed a small smile as she watched Adel turn and leave the room.

***

Though the shops with their plentiful goods had proved a bit of a distraction for Rose, she couldn't fully dispel the melancholy that was swirling inside of her. Part of that came from the heavy reminder hanging around her neck. She hadn't had time to dispose of the dratted thing before leaving on their shopping excursion. She reached up one gloved hand and rubbed the locket methodically.

"Lady Danford," Adel squealed at her side, rousing Rose from her stupor.

Rose's eyes flicked up as Adel rushed to her friend's side. The women embraced excitedly as Rose slinked backward, feeling out of place amidst such merriment.

"What a delight to see you, Lady Rose," Lady Danford cooed as she stepped forward and gifted Rose with a bright smile.

Rose smiled shyly in return. The few times she had met Adel's friend, she had been overcome with her vivaciousness and friendly manner. Today was no different.

"Rose is here to participate in the Season. Isn't that splendid?"

"Truly?" Both of Lady Danford's hands clasped together with glee. "I shall insist on hosting a ball in her honor. This is very exciting news indeed."

Rose didn't want a ball held in her honor, but she was too polite to refuse. "How kind of you," she said instead, though inside she was cringing at the thought of being the center of attention.

Adel and Lady Danford began discussing the details of the ball with great anticipation, leaving Rose to feel like the outsider once more. She decided this was her chance to disappear for a spell, for she couldn't manage to participate in their excitement.

"Excuse me," she interrupted in a quiet voice and was surprised when both women heard her and stopped talking at once. "May I leave you two to the details of the ball while I visit the bookstore and retrieve a new book?"

"Of course," Adel responded.

With a nod of her head, Rose turned and left the shop. Lifting her skirts with one hand, she hurried down towards the bookstore, deciding that some time alone sounded quite splendid at the moment. When she grew depressed, it was nearly impossible for her to enjoy polite company. She wanted nothing more than to be alone with her miserable thoughts.

The smell of paper and ink assaulted her senses as she opened the door to the bookstore. "May I help you, my lady?" a gravelly voice called out at once.

It took her a minute to find the source of the voice. Sitting behind a worn counter was a small, bespectacled man with a hawkish nose and hair as white as snow. "I am here to purchase a book."

The man chuckled as he strode out from behind the counter. "I assumed as much. Is there a particular book you are wanting?"

Rose racked her brain for an answer, but could not think of a single thing. "Uh, not really."

His eyes danced with amusement as he glanced at her over the rims of his spectacles. "Perhaps you'd be interested in a romance novel?"

"No," she spat out quickly, defensively. "I do not care for those types of books. How about a mystery?"

The man tapped his foot in thought before saying, "Follow me, I think I have just the thing."

"Do you mind if I look myself?"

The man paused. "But of course. The mysteries can be found halfway down the third aisle on your right."

Rose nodded her head and began walking towards the isle he had indicated. Truthfully, she wasn't fully interested in finding a book to read; she was merely looking to be left alone. Her gaze flitted over the rows and rows of books, but she didn't stop to inspect a single one. Instead, she kept walking, enjoying the fact that the only noise she heard was the sound of her slippers against the creaky wood floorboards.

Up and down the isles she went, feeling as if she were wandering through a predictable maze. Every once in a while she would reach out and finger the edge of a bookshelf, trailing her gloved finger in the thick layer of dust that was present. She knew she shouldn't do it, for it was dirtying the white silk, but she couldn't resist. It made her feel like she was a kid again, drawing silly pictures in the dust found on the upper shelves of her father's library.

Half way down the next aisle, her nose began to itch. She wiggled it back and forth, trying to relieve the itching, but it was to no avail. Without thinking, she reached her dust covered hand to her nose to scratch and instantly inhaled the dust and began sneezing wildly, in a very unladylike fashion.

Five times she sneezed, a record for her. When she finally stopped, she peeled her gloves from her hands and threw them into her reticule. It was time she be on her way, she thought as she turned to leave the store.

"Excuse me, my lady," a deep voice called out from behind her. Rose startled at the interruption, for she had thought she was alone. Turning, she nearly gasped as she saw Lord deCourtenay standing in the exact spot she had just been.

"You dropped something," he said coolly as his eyes dropped to the ground below.

Rose's eyes followed his and she gasped loudly. There on the floor before him was her locket, laying wide open, the satchel of poison a few inches away. It must have come loose during her violent sneezing fit. She dropped to her knees to retrieve it, but Lord deCourtenay did the same, snatching the locket and poison up in one large hand.

"Give that to me," she commanded, though it did not escape her that her voice was shaking pathetically.

He rose and inspected the contents in his hands. One brow rose curiously above his serious green eyes. "Arsenic?" he questioned without a hint of amusement.

Rose lunged, but Lord deCourtenay took a step away from her, refusing to give her belongings back. "That belongs to me," she hissed. "If you do not return it to my possession at once, I will alert the clerk that you have stolen something of mine."

"I have every intent of giving it back," he snapped. "What I am curious to know, however, is why a lady would need to carry a satchel of poison on her person. Have you any plans to use it?"

"Of course not."

"Then why even carry it? It would be dangerous for it to fall into the wrong hands."

"Such as yours?"

He gave a derisive laugh. "I can assure you that I am no murderer."

"And I can assure you that neither am I."

He stalked towards her then, slowly, deliberately. That intense stare of his boring into her, making her squirm. What was it about this man that caused such discomfort? She began taking timid steps away from him.

"Are you scared of me?" he asked, never looking away.

"You unnerve me, my lord," she admitted truthfully. "Every time I have encountered you, I am left feeling as if you do not trust me."

"Because I don't."

"Though I have done nothing to warrant such opinion?" she asked, somewhat hurt by his admission.

"Do not act as if my opinion matters to you. We both know that it doesn't."

Rose swallowed against the lump forming in her throat. "The last time we talked, you insisted you were my friend. Had that all been a lie?"

She watched curiously as his near hateful stare softened and his shoulders slumped. "I wasn't lying."

"Then why are you treating me with disdain?"

He was silent for a long time before admitting, "I suppose learning that you carry around a satchel of poison has caught me a bit off-guard."

"I meant to get rid of it."

"In a gentleman's glass of brandy?"

Rose wanted to slap him for his accusation. "No, in the river Thames. I never want to see that wretched thing again. It's truthfully none of your business, but since you are looking at me like I am guilty of some horrendous crime, I will enlighten you. That locket, including the poison, was given to me by my late husband on our wedding night."

Lord deCourtenay made to interrupt, but she stopped him by thrusting one shaking hand up in front of her. "No, let me finish. He gave it to me and told me that it was the only way I would ever be free of him. Do you get my meaning? My husband," she spat out angrily, "told me that I would have to kill myself in order to get away from his abuse. The reason I never got rid of it, is because I honestly considered using it more than once. You have no idea what kind of man he was or what kind of hell he made me endure, so stop staring at me as if I'm some evil person capable of murder when it was him who was the monster, not me."

Her chest was heaving violently by the time she was done with her impassioned speech. She nearly expected the shopkeeper to come ask her to lower her voice, but he didn't.

Several long drawn out seconds passed before Lord deCourtenay stretched forth his hand and stroked her cheek. She inhaled sharply in surprise. The pad of his thumb trailed methodically down her cheek, causing a strange tingling sensation to course through her.

"What are you doing?" she tried to snap, but his touch had rendered her voice weak.

"I'm thinking about kissing you."

His husky voice washed over her as she closed her eyes and breathed, "I've never been kissed before." It stunned her how easily her anger had been displaced by merely a touch of his hand.

"Impossible. You were married."

"I've never been kissed before, not by a man that didn't mean to harm me."

Her head was spinning. Why was she admitting things to him that she had never admitted to another human being? Why wasn't she running from him? Instead, she just stood there, her lips slightly parted in anticipation of his kiss.

"I would never harm you," he whispered as his breath fanned her face, and oddly enough, she believed him.

***

Cameron felt as if his whole world had been turned upside-down. He was holding a satchel of arsenic in his hand, poison that had come from the lady's own locket, and instead of being incredibly suspicious of her, he found himself believing her emotional admission.

She was fragile, she was scarred, and she was maddeningly vulnerable, a heady combination that tugged at his heart strings. At that moment, he couldn't resist her. He dropped the locket and poison and cupped her face with his hands as he pushed her back into the bookshelf and fitted his body to hers. His head lowered slowly as her eyelashes fluttered against her cheeks in anticipation. He longed to show her what a real kiss should be.

His lips pressed against hers, and he groaned when she responded with a much-unexpected eagerness. He felt as if he had waited his whole life for her kiss. His hands slid to her slender neck where he felt her pulse beating wildly beneath her skin. When her hands went timidly to his chest, he had to refrain from consuming her, reminding himself that they were in a very public location.

He forced himself to act like a gentleman, though he felt anything but, and somehow managed to pull away. He bent and retrieved the locket and poison and thrust it into her palm. "Take it," he urged when her fingers refused to clasp around it.

"I don't want it. I don't want anything that reminds me of him."

He let the locket slide back into his palm as his fingers clasped around it. "I will dispose of it for you."

78

"Thank you," she said through trembling lips, lips that were swollen from his kiss.

"Rose, there you are."

Both of them turned in alarm as Lady Straton turned the corner. Cameron took a hasty step away from Rose as heat crept up the back of his neck.

"Have you found a book yet?" Lady Straton asked with sincerity, the polite smile never leaving her face. Cameron was grateful that she acted as if it were normal to find them alone like that.

"Uh, yes," Rose stammered as she turned from him and grabbed the first book she could find. Thrusting it towards her sister-in-law, she said, "This is the one I came for. Lord deCourtenay was so kind to show me where it was."

"How kind indeed." Hooking their arms together, Lady Straton turned to him, "Thank you for your assistance. Good day."

Cameron bowed slightly before the women then watched as the two sauntered off towards the front of the shop to purchase the book, the locket and poison clasped tightly in his grasp. His next stop would be the Thames where he would throw the painful reminder into the river where it would never haunt her again.

Chapter Nine

The beginning of the season always brought the biggest crowds to any party, and being that the Gilbert's ballroom was on the small side, the crush of people seemed even more overwhelming than normal. The stifling heat from all those dancing bodies was enough to make Rose want to leave, but the hope of seeing Lord deCourtenay caused her to persevere. Standing on the sidelines, she fanned her face furiously as her sharp gaze took in her surroundings. Her eyes had been shifting about the crowds all night, hoping to catch a glimpse of Cameron. Since their unexpected kiss in the bookstore, she had been unable to think of much else.

"I've been looking for you all evening," the low voice behind her purred.

Rose felt the hairs on the back of her neck stand as she at once recognized Lord deCourtenay's voice. "I've been here for hours, leading me to believe that your efforts to find me have been weak."

Cameron chuckled as he came to stand by her side. "There are hundreds of people crammed into this small room; it's not easy to move about freely."

"No, it is not," Rose agreed as a gentleman passing by accidentally bumped into her, causing her to stumble into Cameron. His hands went up to steady her at once, holding her close. Rose's face blushed at the contact.

"I would ask you to dance, but there is hardly room to move about. Care to accompany me to the balcony for some fresh air."

Rose looked around, hoping to find Adel to seek her permission, but she couldn't see her sister-in-law anywhere. Hadn't she just been by her side? Seeing the look of concern on her face, Cameron was quick to point out, "Perhaps your chaperone has gone to get some fresh air as well." Taking her arm and linking it through his he began to move slowly through the people towards the balcony. "If we do not find her, I promise I will not keep you long. But you cannot deny that some cold air is much needed at the moment."

"That I cannot," she sighed. Something about the man made her feel unusually at ease.

When they finally approached the balcony, Rose couldn't help but laugh; it was crammed with people seeking the same relief they were. There was hardly room for them amongst all the people milling about. "It would seem we are destined to get no relief from the heat."

"That isn't true. Come, follow me."

Without a second thought, Rose turned and followed Cameron as he shouldered his way through the throngs. He led her out of the ballroom and down a long hall filled with paintings to where a pair of French doors led to another small balcony, one that apparently, no one else was aware of, for it was blissfully empty.

"How'd you know this was here?" she asked in awe as the first delicious wave of cold air hit her warm skin.

"I found it while looking for you."

"Why were you searching for me?" she asked with a hint of hopefulness lacing her words. She had long ago lost her ability to anticipate much good coming her way, but after their kiss, she couldn't keep herself from dreaming of him, of dreaming of something she had decided she'd never have. Hidden deep within her was the desire to be loved and cherished, the desire for companionship.

His gaze turned on her, solemn and unreadable. "I wanted to apologize. I should never have accused you of ulterior motives when I found the poison."

"It was only natural to suspect something was afoot. How many people make it a habit of carrying arsenic around on their person?" she said with a small laugh, though she was truly grateful for his apology. It had hurt her to think he thought her capable of such a horrendous crime.

"Your husband must have been a monster."

Rose snorted, "An understatement, my lord. He was the vilest person I have ever had the misfortune of knowing." Without realizing it, her slight frame began to shake.

Cameron stepped forward, placing both of his hands on her trembling shoulders. "Why did you marry him?"

"My father arranged the match shortly after my mother died. I assume it was so he wouldn't have to deal with me going about my first season."

"Did he know what kind of a man Lord Moncrief was?"

For a brief moment, she wondered how he knew her late husband's name, for she was certain she had never spoken it to him before. But alas, people gossiped, and she was certain she was the topic on more than one occasion.

Rose shrugged her shoulders, though it was a hard task under the weight of his heavy palms. "I would like to think he didn't, but I cannot be sure."

"Have you never asked him?"

She shook her head sadly, "No, I haven't spoken to him since my wedding. I still haven't forgiven him for what he did to me."

"I think that is quite understandable." His voice was low, "You have every reason not to trust a man, for you have been hurt on too many occasions."

His hands wandered from her shoulders and were now cupping her face ever so gently. "I want you to trust me."

"Why," she breathed airily, unable to think clearly when he was touching her.

"Because I can keep you safe."

"Safe? Safe from what? I no longer live my life in fear of anybody, not since my husband's death."

"Good," he muttered sincerely as he leaned forward and pressed a tender kiss to her brow.

She breathed deeply of his scent, relishing the way she felt protected in his presence. She couldn't remember ever feeling so safe with a gentleman before. Perhaps that is why she allowed herself to tilt her face towards him, parting her lips as her eyes fluttered closed in anticipation of his kiss.

His words came softly as his warm breath snaked across her skin, "I best return you to the ballroom. I do not wish to have your brother call me out."

"I wouldn't allow that to happen," she said with conviction as her eyes snapped open.

Cameron chuckled. "I daresay that if your brother wanted to call me out, there would be nothing you could do to stop him."

"That isn't true. Griffin wouldn't do anything to upset me."

Rose stared into his muted green eyes, refusing to look away. Again, it wasn't the color that drew her in; it was the intensity of his gaze as he spoke, "Would it upset you greatly if he did indeed call me out?"

"Of course it would," she said with a measure of exasperation. "Why?"

His voice was low and husky, causing her to tingle. He was so handsome, nothing at all like her late husband. And the way he looked at her was as foreign to her as any modicum of kindness had been during her marriage. "Because," she began before hesitating, her eyes drifting downward, away from his.

She felt his warm hand beneath her chin, drawing her face upwards. "Because why?"

Her heart beat wildly as she contemplated telling him the truth. She had learned long ago that it was best to keep her true feelings a secret, lest she be punished for them. It was as if he could read her mind. "Darling," he whispered, "you don't have to be afraid to tell me."

Averting her gaze once more, she admitted, "I'm beginning to care for you."

Unfortunately, since she still refused to look at him, Rose missed the broad smile that broke out on his face at her admission. "That pleases me."

Rose looked up at him, a bit of wonder mixed with skepticism on her face. "Does it, my lord?"

"Greatly," he breathed as he pulled her close, his head lowering so his lips could find hers. The kiss was brief, but just as magical as the first, leading Rose to believe that, indeed, there was something different about his man.

She wasn't entirely ready for the kiss to end when it did, but Cameron pulled back and muttered, "I have to return you to the ballroom."

This time she understood his insistence, for she knew if she spent much more time alone with him, she would be ruined.

***

"I'm convinced she is not a murderer."

Andrew leaned forward across the desk; his eyes scrunched into skeptical slits. "And we are convinced that she is. What proof do you

86

have otherwise?"

Cameron inhaled deeply as his thumbs drummed rhythmically against his breeches-clad thighs. How was he going to explain to his better that the only proof he had was a hunch? "I have yet to gather any concrete evidence, but my instincts tell me we best start looking elsewhere if we hope to find the true murderer."

"Your instincts?" Andrew drawled, unamused. "Are your instincts always correct?"

The man's doubt caused Cameron's pride to prickle. "Have I ever failed at any assignment I have been given?" Without waiting for an answer, he continued, "Either you trust me to do the job, or you find another man. I promise results, but I expect nothing less than your implicit trust as I go about determining who the real killer is."

"I wouldn't be so hasty to—"

Just then another man came barging through the door, interrupting their conversation without an apology. His eyes flicked towards Cameron before returning to Andrew. "There's been another murder. Lord Gilbert was found dead just this morning. His wife claims that he retired early from the party they were hosting at their townhouse, stating he was tired and the loud music was giving him a headache. She swears that was the last time she saw him alive."

Cameron's jaw tensed at the news, for he knew without having to look, that Lord Gilbert was on the list of men he had been given at the very beginning of the case. "Are you certain his death is a result of murder and not due to natural causes?"

"Yes, indeed, my lord, for the doctor was called in to investigate and he determined that Lord Gilbert had been poisoned."

"Of course he had." Andrew leaned forward across his desk as he exhaled loudly, his eyes boring deeply into Cameron's. "You better rethink your hunch. Something tells me that our suspect had something to do with this. Was she at that party?" he asked pointedly.

A pit formed in the bottom of Cameron's stomach. He didn't believe that Rose was a killer. There had to be some other excuse for the string of murder's that kept pointing to her as the culprit. "Yes, she was there."

"Somehow I already knew it," Andrew said smugly, causing Cameron to bristle with irritation. "I strongly suggest that you stop letting a pretty face distract you from your job."

If his earlier words had irritated Cameron, this last statement nearly made him furious. That was not what he was doing.

Or was it?

Cameron played back every encounter he'd had with Rose over and over in his mind as his carriage rolled along the crowded streets of London towards the Straton's townhouse. This was not the first assignment he had been given involving a pretty face, in fact, Rose's beauty was easily overshadowed by some of the more wicked women who had been heavily involved in elaborate crimes over the years. Not once had he let his guard down around those other more experienced, more provocative women, though many had tried to lure him in with their charms.

What was it about Rose that had him turned inside out? He thought back to the pain he saw each time he gazed into her dark eyes and he wondered if her vulnerability was what had him so jumbled. Did he simply feel sorry for the girl? No, that wasn't it, he thought indignantly, for he had been trained not to allow even the most heart-wrenching of emotions to affect his work.

Blast it all; he had to put aside whatever strange feelings he harbored for the girl and do his job. There was a murderer on the loose, and it was his job to stop them. Though he was certain Rose was not the person they were looking for, his budding feelings for the chit were interfering with his work. He could not allow it to continue.

Cameron forced his breathing to slow as he alighted from his carriage and bounded up the stairs leading to the Straton's townhouse. He knocked loudly before stretching his neck from side to side to relieve the tension he was carrying. As soon as he handed the butler his card, he was shown inside. He expected to find Lady Rose in the drawing room, accepting her morning callers, but the room was empty.

Several seconds had passed before Lord Straton appeared in the room. For a moment, Cameron wondered if he had come to call him out. Had Rose told him of the kiss they had shared yesterday? He had to force his eyes from lowering in shame at the thought.

"Lord deCourtenay, my butler informs me that you are here to call on Rose."

"Yes, that is correct."

"I regret to inform you she has been called away for a time."

Cameron couldn't hide his disappointment, his eyes narrowing into slits. Would it be too bold of him to ask where she was? "I hope that all is well."

Lord Straton let out a long sigh as he signaled for Cameron to sit. He folded his large frame into the settee across from him as he waited patiently for him to speak.

"She has gone to visit our father, though only the devil would know why."

"When did she leave?"

"Before dawn, if you can believe it. One would think a long night of dancing would have kept her in bed a bit longer, but I can't pretend to understand my sister or her motives, especially where my father is concerned. If I were her, I'd never want to see the man again."

The venomous anger in Lord Straton's words didn't surprise Cameron one bit, for he practically hated the man too for what he did to Rose, and he had never even met him. "How long do you anticipate she will be gone?"

"That I do not know. My father's missive stated that he has taken ill. He has summoned Rose to him because he is on his deathbed."

"Do you think he means to apologize?" Cameron asked without thinking.

Lord Straton eyed him curiously, "I presume Rose has told you about the wonderful man my father is?" he bit out sarcastically.

"More or less."

"Then you will understand why I believe an apology will never be forthcoming. The man does not have it in him to feel sorry for anyone other than himself. He will never admit that his actions were wrong, you can mark my words. No, I do not think he intends to apologize to

Rose, I believe he has called for her in hopes that she would take care of him during his illness."

"Would she?" he asked curiously.

Lord Straton looked at him; his dark brows scrunched together, "I'm not entirely sure. In the past, I would have easily answered no, but her leaving so suddenly has me confused. Perhaps she will." Then, shaking his head in wonder, he muttered, "The opposite sex confuses me greatly. Are all woman so complicated?"

Cameron shrugged his shoulders, "You, my lord, would know more than me. I haven't any sisters or a wife with which to draw experience from."

"Someday that will change, at least the wife part."

"Until then, I will continue to enjoy my peace," Cameron said as he pasted a carefree smile on his face and stood. "I best be on my way. I will wait for Lady Rose to return before bothering you with my presence again."

"It is no bother," Lord Straton answered honestly. "You are welcome anytime."

The minute Cameron left the townhouse; the forced smile left his face. Blast it all, why did Rose have to leave right now? It was the worst possible timing. Her departure would only make her look more suspect, fleeing from Town right after another murder was committed. He knew she had nothing to do with it, but her actions would not appear innocent. Perhaps he could catch up with her and convince her to return to London before anyone noticed her absence.

Chapter 10

Manhall Manor had only changed for the worst during her long
absence. The staff was minimal, which could account for the poor
upkeep and the draftiness that pervaded every room. Rose shivered as
she pulled her shawl tightly around her shoulders, willing herself not
to tremble as she was shown into the drawing-room upon her arrival.

Sitting on the edge of a wing-backed chair, she listened to the clock
tick away the seconds as her anxiety rose with each annoying click.
Why had she come? She asked herself for the hundredth time. Was
she truly expecting her father to apologize to her for forcing her to
wed the monster, Lord Moncrief? She scoffed at the thought,
realistically knowing that his apology was not likely, though, in her
heart of hearts, that is what had provoked her to come. Deep down,
she longed for an explanation. She wanted to see contrition upon her
father's face as he told her he was sorry for causing her so much pain.

"Your father will see you in his chamber." The monotone voice of the butler intruded upon her thoughts, causing her to startle.

Rose inhaled deeply before rising. In a few moments, she would know why she had been summoned. As she followed behind the butler, her hand dropped to her side, subconsciously looking for Prince so she could wind her fingers in his thick fur. She wanted to weep when her hand met with nothing but cold emptiness. She'd had to leave Prince behind at her brother's townhouse, which saddened her greatly. She could really use him now. His overwhelming presence always calmed her.

Pushing the door of her father's bedchamber open, the butler gestured her inside. With trepidation, she went. She only had a moment to notice and be grateful for the roaring fire burning in the hearth before her thoughts were intruded upon by her father's familiar voice. "You came."

Rose stopped in her tracks, her eyes searching for her father in the dark recesses of the canopied bed. "Yes," she said shakily. When her response was met with only silence, she asked, "Why did you summon me here?"

Without any emotion, her father explained, "I'm dying, Rose. I need someone to care for me."

Rose scoffed, "You have servants who could see to your care. You didn't need to call me here."

"Here I lay on my deathbed and wish only to be surrounded by family. Have you no sympathy for me?"

Truth be told, she didn't. The anger and betrayal she had tried hard to tamper down over the years came bubbling to the surface. "How can you expect sympathy from me when you never showed me even an ounce of such emotion in my entire life?" she wailed, wishing she could see his face more clearly as she spoke.

"I do not know what you mean," he said flatly. Then, ignoring her little outburst, he asked, "Did Griffin come with you?"

"No, he refused," she quipped curtly.

"That ungrateful bas—"

Rose quickly cut off the insult. "I should have listened to him when he begged me not to come as well. He told me you hadn't changed, but for some reason, I had to come see for myself."

"How would he know anything about me?" her father growled. "He hasn't come to see me for more than five years."

"And you never bothered to visit him either. You didn't even attend his wedding or come for his children's births. You're a grandfather now, though you might not even be aware of that fact."

For the briefest of moments, Rose believed she saw something akin to sadness flick across her father's face, but it was quickly replaced by his cold, stony resolve. "I don't know what I ever did to deserve such ungrateful, uncaring children."

Rose was taken back by his comment. She almost laughed at the absurdity of his statement, had it not angered her so. Her shawl dropped from her shoulders as she stiffened before him, ready to finally tell him how she really felt. "I have to admit that I'm grateful you are confined to your bed, for I have some things to say to you and I do not wish you to walk away. 'What have you done to deserve such ungrateful, uncaring children?'" she repeated his question back to him, "Well let me tell you. You have been cold and aloof our entire lives. You treated mother as if she was less than one of your servants, ignoring her existence though she never did anything to warrant your coldness. Your treatment of Griffin and myself was not much better. I can't recall you ever spending time with us or engaging us in conversation for the intent of getting to know us better, of establishing a relationship with us. But all of that could have been overlooked had you not forced me into a loveless, abusive, nightmare of a marriage to the Baron Moncrief. That, Father, is why Griffin hates you. While he was forced to witness the horrendous circumstances my awful marriage left me in, you stayed locked up in your mansion, pretending as if nothing untoward was occurring. You are a despicable excuse for a father, for you should never have allowed such atrociousness to occur."

Rose's chest was heaving violently after her outburst. Her whole body was shaking, but it was high time she told her father what she really thought of him. She expected his anger, but it never came.

In a cold, emotionless voice he asked, "So Griffin hates me? What about you, Rose? Do you hate me as well?"

"Yes," she spit out without having to think. "I do."

"Very well. I can see that it was a mistake to ask you to come. I will allow you to spend the night since the hour is late, but I will expect you to leave at first light. As long as I'm living, I do not wish to see you or your pathetic brother at Manhall Manor ever again."

That was it? Her father was kicking her out of his house, of his life?

Had the man no feelings? Could he not feel even a hint of regret for his actions and behavior that had caused so much heartache and pain? She stood in awe, staring at the miserable, unfeeling man she called Father. She debated saying more, but approaching footsteps behind her prevented it.

"Lady Rose, allow me to show you to your bedchamber."

She didn't want to stay the night in the dratted place, but she knew it would be unwise to travel at this late hour. Without another word to her father, she turned and left the bedchamber, wishing she had been smart enough to listen to Griffin and never had come.

***

The minute the door of her bedchamber closed behind her, Rose dissolved into tears. She threw herself across the bed and wept, loud sobs racking her entire being. She didn't simply cry for herself either, she also cried painful tears for her dear brother and her poor mother, the two people she loved most in her life who had been victims of her father's cruelty as well.

She wasn't sure how long she laid there crying but was startled out of her despair when she heard a loud squeaking sound. Inhaling sharply, she sat up on the bed and glanced at the window as a body crawled through. She was paralyzed with fear, unsure of what to do when the man stood up straight, adjusted his clothes, and turned to face her. She nearly swooned when her eyes settled on the familiar face of Lord deCourtenay.

"Cameron," she exclaimed, "what are you doing here?"

"Coming to take you back to London," he said as he took a step towards her.

"Whatever for?" Not that she wasn't grateful and ready to leave Manhall Manor, but she couldn't understand why he was there. "Did Griffin send you?"

"No, I came of my own accord. There's something I need to tell you."

Rose tried to wait patiently for his explanation, but when none seemed forthcoming, she snapped, "Well, do not keep me waiting. Whatever you have to tell me must be of utmost importance for you to sneak into my father's home at this late hour."

"It really is. Rose," he said as he drew closer, "I've been working as a secret agent since my return from the war." She gasped, but he only continued, "And you, my dear, are suspected of murder."

"No, it can't be true." Nothing was making any sense to her. Perhaps she was merely caught in one of her disturbing nightmares. "If it were, you wouldn't be telling me. Aren't secret agents supposed to keep their identity hidden?"

His reached for her, drawing her to him. She didn't object for she was secretly grateful that his strong embrace was there to steady her, for she felt like she could collapse. "Normally, yes, that is the protocol. There have been a string of murders occurring in London, and the one thing they have in common is a tie to your late husband. Apparently, all of the men who have been killed had, at one point in time, won a significant amount of money from Lord Moncrief. The Main Office suspects you are involved in these crimes and has hired me to investigate."

"Cameron, I'm not a murderer," she said as her dark eyes bore into his. She must make him understand that she would never do something like that. "I promise you that I have never killed another person. Do you believe me?"

"I do," he said with conviction as his grip on her tightened. "I went to the Main Office just this morning to tell them that I did not think you were behind these crimes when they informed me that Lord Gilbert was murdered last night." Rose sucked in a startled breath. "My betters are not convinced that you are not involved, and I had no proof to offer them of your innocence. When I learned you had fled Town, I knew I had to find you and bring you back. Your absence is incriminating."

"I didn't flee town," she said indignantly. "I was summoned here by my father. I have the missive to prove it."

She pulled away and made to find it. Cameron drew her back to him. "Rose, I don't need proof, I believe you. What I need is for you to cooperate. I have a carriage waiting that is prepared to drive through the night to deliver you safely back to London. Once there, we have to figure out who the true killer is before anything happens to you."

A chill coursed down her spine. "You told me you could keep me safe."

"And I can, but I need you to listen to what I say. You will return to London, and you will go about the Season as if nothing untoward has happened. There will be no mention of this brief visit. I will inform you of places and people I need you to avoid while I continue my investigation. Several people had taken a significant amount of blunt from your husband, and I do not want you anywhere near them. If one of them ends up dead, there will be no connection that can be made to you. Understand?" When she shook her head yes, he continued, "And you absolutely cannot, under any circumstance, utter a word of this to anyone. No one can know of my work as a secret agent, and no one can know of my involvement with this case. Can you promise me that you will keep it a secret?"

"Of course."

"Good, now hurry and gather your things so we can be on our way."

Rose turned to do just that but then quickly turned back to Cameron. "How did you know I was innocent?"

"I have excellent intuition. That's why I make such a good secret agent." His proud smile made him all the more appealing.

"Very impressive, my lord."

"As much as I'd like to bask in your admiration, we truly must get going."

Rose nodded and quickly grabbed her shawl then gestured to her small trunk. "This is mine as well. I wasn't certain how long I'd be staying."

Cameron hefted the trunk into his arms, seemingly unaware of its weight. "Let's be off."

"Surely we aren't going out the window," she muttered as she glanced uneasily at the window behind him.

"Of course not. We will simply walk out the front door."

Rose felt a bit foolish for not thinking of the obvious. She held the door open and let Cameron carry the trunk through before squeezing past him to lead the way. The halls were dark and cold. Rose wished she had thought to bring a candle with her to light their path. They traveled slowly. Though the hallways were familiar to Rose, they didn't seem quite the same in the eerie darkness.

As fate would have it, just as they were approaching her father's bedchamber, Cameron's boot caught on the rug causing him to stumble. The trunk he was carrying fell from his arms and hit the ground with a loud bang. Rose cringed as he hurried and picked up the trunk.

"What is going on here?"

Rose froze as her father's voice boomed loudly from his now open doorway. She squared her shoulders and tried to act brave. "We are leaving, just as you wished."

"We? Who is with you? I thought you traveled here alone."

Before she could answer, Cameron stepped forth and said, "Pleased to meet you, I'm Lord deCourtenay."

Her father eyed him shrewdly. "Are you her husband?"

"Uh, no," Cameron answered while Rose blushed at his question.

"Then what are you doing with my daughter in the middle of the night? Have you been in her chamber?"

"Father," Rose interrupted, "nothing untoward has occurred. Lord deCourtenay is simply helping me return to London."

"Silence, child. I did not address you," he barked rudely. "Lord deCourtenay, have your or have you not been in my daughter's chamber?"

"Well yes, but like Rose said, nothing happened. I merely went to gather her and retrieve her trunk."

"I have servants for that sort of thing. I do not believe that you are as innocent as you claim." Looking between the pair he muttered, "I believe something havey cavey is going on here."

"Sir, I can assure you that is not the case."

"And I can assure you that I do not believe you."

"Father," Rose pleaded, "just let us leave. You said I am no longer welcome here, so surely you should have no problem allowing us to be on our way."

"Not before I insist that this man makes this right. He has compromised you under my roof. As your father, I have only one option—force him to wed you."

Chapter Eleven

Rose was thrust back in time, to the day her father told her, in all brusqueness, that she would, in no uncertain terms, wed the Baron Moncrief. Though she felt her insides coil with dread, she managed to find her voice, "Father, you cannot dictate who I will wed. Not this time."

"I am your father and will do as I wish."

Cameron surprised Rose by interjecting, "You can't force me to wed your daughter, sir, for I am ready to do it willingly."

Rose's mouth hung open as she looked at him strangely. "What are you saying?"

Cameron turned to her then, compassion shining through his eyes. "Rose, I am willing to wed you to make things right, to appease your father."

"I have reached the age of majority, he cannot dictate who I will wed," she cried with exasperation. "And there is nothing to make right; we did nothing wrong."

Cameron turned to her father and said indignantly, "The lady is correct, sir."

Her father's face was unreadable until his eyes scrunched into angry slits. Rose was certain he did not like being defied. "Get out," he roared loudly, causing the hairs on the back of her arms to rise.

Though for a brief moment Rose wanted to try and smooth things over with her father, she was wise enough to know that it would do no good. Grabbing the hem of her skirt, she shouldered past Cameron and nearly ran from the house, biting back bitter tears as she did so.

Just like Cameron had promised, there was a carriage waiting. She flung the door open and dashed inside, wanting to put some separation between her and the house that held so many painful memories. Just when she was about to let the pent-up tears free, Cameron appeared in the carriage, her trunk still in his hands. She turned her knees to the side so he could push it inside, then waited for him to take a seat.

"I should show you how a father is supposed to act." His jaw twitched angrily, and it touched her that he was so affected by her father's behavior.

"What do you mean?"

Those intent green eyes of his settled upon her. "Your father is a tyrant, a miserable wretch of a man. Men are not supposed to feel hate towards those he has sired. My father would never think twice of treating his offspring in such a manner."

Her lip trembled as she asked, "Do you think my father truly hates me?"

He released a slow breath before moving to her side of the carriage and taking her hands into his own. "Rose, I think your father hates himself, and he's only reflecting that hatred upon you. I don't see how it could be possible for anyone to hate you."

The lump in her throat burned from trying to keep her emotions at bay. She finally felt the hot tears begin to stream down her cheeks and she didn't bother stopping them. "My husband hated me. I couldn't provide him with an heir and it infuriated him."

"That should not incite hatred. Disappointment is understandable; hatred is unwarranted. 'Tis not your fault that God did not place a child in your womb."

"But he did, five of them to be exact, but my body wasn't strong enough to carry them. I'm too thin, and I spent too much time walking in the gardens."

Cameron was staring at her in dismay. "You don't believe that, do you? There are plenty of women just as thin as you, or more so, that have born children, and walking too much should not have caused you to lose your babies. Your head has been filled with rubbish, my dear, utter rubbish."

"Do you sincerely believe that?"

"Absolutely," he scoffed. "You cannot carry the burden of responsibility for what has happened."

Rose let his words sink in. Realistically she knew that her losses were not her fault, but deep down she had always wondered. She could still hear her husband's belittling voice hurling insults at her, blaming her for every one of their misfortunes, though it was likely that his abuse was the cause of their losses, not something she had done.

Cameron urged her head to his shoulder, "Rest, my dear, and try to forget about tonight's awful events. I will protect you from your father and any other person who means you harm; you can count on it."

She wasn't entirely sure why, but Rose believed him. It wasn't often that she felt safe and secure, but with him, she always had. This assurance allowed her to fall quickly to sleep.

***

The poor woman in his arms had evoked more feelings in him this night than anyone else had during his lifetime. Cameron was grateful that Lord Moncrief was dead, for he'd kill him with his own bare hands if it meant keeping Rose safe. The thought of anyone harming her made his blood boil angrily inside of him. She had been mistreated by too many people , and he would not be one of them. He vowed to do everything in his power to not only keep her safe but to secure her affections and show her how a true gentleman was supposed to behave.

When the carriage pulled up in front to the Straton's townhouse, Rose was still fast asleep. He scooped her into his arms and alighted effortlessly from the carriage. The sun was still buried behind the horizon, and Cameron was certain the entire household was asleep. He attempted to turn the door handle, but it was locked, so he knocked loudly, hating the fact that he was rousing the household.

As he waited for someone to awake and answer the door, Cameron stood silently, observing the woman in his arms. She was not much bigger than a child, but though she was small, her body was perfectly formed as a woman's should be. Her thick, dark lashes fluttered softly against her pale cheeks, and he wondered if she were dreaming.

"What is going on here?"

Cameron's eyes settled upon a confused looking Lord Straton, a banyan wrapped around his person; his hair disheveled from sleep. "I will explain everything as soon as I'm allowed to enter and deposit your sister in her bed."

Lord Straton swung the door open and allowed him inside. He led him to the second floor where Rose's chamber was and pulled back the bed coverings. Cameron laid her gently atop the mattress then pulled the covers up over her body. Prince bounded atop the bed and laid his large body right next to his mistress. Cameron smiled as she reached her arm around the beast in her sleep. It made him happy to see how much she cared for the dog that had once been his.

It wasn't until they were seated in Lord Straton's study that Cameron began to explain his unexpected appearance. "I went to Manhall Manor to speak with your sister and discovered that your father was treating her abhorrently."

Lord Straton cut him off, "Why in the devil would you go to Manhall Manor? Why not simply wait for my sister to return?"

This is the part he would have to lie about, for he could not tell Lord Straton the truth. His duty as a secret agent very much depended on secrecy, and he was unwilling to tell one more person about his assignment; hence he risk jeopardizing the mission. Pasting a lopsided grin on his face, he explained, "I must confess that the thought of waiting for you sister to return seemed like agony to my anxious soul. I was uncertain how long the wait would be, and I couldn't fathom prolonging my proposal for even one more day."

Lord Straton choked. "Your proposal? Did I hear you correctly?"

Cameron twined his fingers together and placed them on his knee. "Yes, my lord, you did. I fled to Manhall Manor with the intent of seeking Rose's hand in marriage."

Running his hands through his hair, Lord Straton shook his head as if to clear it. "I wasn't aware of your intentions towards Rose. Please tell me if your mission was successful."

"In a sense. I did make my intentions known to Rose, though she has yet to accept my proposal. Your father attempted to use force to persuade her to accept, but I refused to allow that to happen. I do not want her becoming my wife unless it's of her own free will. I assume you know how tyrannical your father can be, which proved to upset Rose greatly. I told her she did not have to remain at Manhall Manor and be subject to that. Hence, the reason we traveled through the night to return. Being in your father's presence was extremely upsetting to Rose."

"I tried to dissuade her from going, for I knew the effect he has on her, on anyone he comes in contact with, really."

"Well she is home now, and I will continue to court her until she decides to accept my proposal or turns down my offer of marriage."

Lord Straton looked at him long and hard before issuing the

warning, "Do not attempt to coerce Rose, for I will not allow a marriage to occur unless I'm satisfied it's what she wants and it's what will be best for her."

"Fair enough. Now, if you will allow me to excuse myself, it has been a long night, and I best be on my way home."

Cameron left the Straton townhouse entirely sure that his story had been believed, though he wasn't quite certain how he'd inform Rose of the change in story or precisely how he would get out of the mock proposal, or if he even wanted to. But Cameron was clever, and that's why he had been hired on as a secret agent. He could figure things out that not many could, and right now he had his fair share of dilemmas to solve.

Chapter Twelve

Rose awoke nestled in her own bed, next to the warm, furry body of Prince. How she had gotten there, she wasn't sure, but she was glad that she was home. The events of the previous night felt like a distant nightmare. Was she even certain any of it had actually happened?

She rang a bell to summon her ladies maid then went and sat at her dressing table. Laying on the table was a folded piece of parchment sealed with a drop of wax. She quickly broke the seal and read:

Lady Rose,

I was forced to explain my presence last night to your brother. I knew that I couldn't tell him the truth, so I informed him that my reason for going to Manhall Manor was to seek your hand in marriage. I have convinced him that I was acting like a lovestruck lad and that your father attempted to force your hand, though that was unacceptable to both of us.

Suffice it to say; your brother now thinks that I am courting you in an attempt to win your hand. This will work to our advantage as we strive to work together to discover who the true murderer is and clear your good name. I need you to assist me in this charade for the time being, as our true purpose cannot be made known. Please see that this letter is burned upon completion of reading it, so that no one will discover the truth.
My regards,
Lord deCourtenay

Rose folded the letter, surprised at the disappointment that filled her breast. She was a bit bothered by his formal address. Last night he had held her, comforted her, and even told her father that he was willing to wed her, and today he wrote to her as if everything between them was merely a business deal.

She quickly discarded the missive into the fireplace then returned to her table just as her maid entered the room, followed closely by Adel. The smile on her sister-in-law's face made Rose suspicious.

Her maid began brushing through her hair as she asked, "Why do you appear so happy this morning?"

"Griffin has told me that Lord deCourtenay wishes to court you."

She had never been an exceptionally good actress, but she pasted on a smile nonetheless and replied, "Yes, he does."

Adel squealed in delight. "He's so handsome and kind."

She didn't have to lie when she said, "Yes, he is."

"Do you suppose he'll call on you today?"

"I am uncertain."

"Well regardless, I think we should go to Bond Street and purchase you a new bonnet to celebrate."

Laughing, Rose turned in her chair to look at Adel. "What a frivolous notion. My dressing room is full of fripperies that you and Griffin have purchased for me. I do not need another item to add to the collection." The look Adel was giving her indicated she did not wish to argue.

Approximately an hour later, Rose found herself being dragged to all of Adel's favorite shops. Truth be told, the enjoyment her sister-in-law got from purchasing items was a bit contagious. She allowed herself to forget about the fact that the Main Office suspected her of murder and the fact that Cameron was now pretending to court her, and she found that she was truly enjoying herself.

"Do you know what I was thinking the other night at the Gilbert's ball?" Adel asked her as they strolled arm in arm.

"No, what is that?"

"That you would look simply stunning in a coquelicot gown. Let us venture to Madame Gillrey's and see if she has time to fit you for one."

"Coquelicot is far too bold a color."

Adel merely rolled her eyes at her weak protests and pulled her along. When they entered Madame Gillrey's shop, they didn't have to wait long to be greeted. The petite lady excused herself from the conversation she was having with another customer and came at once to their side.

"Lady Straton, Lady Rose, what brings you to my shop this fine day?"

Adel answered for them, "I would like you to fit Rose for a ballgown."

Madame Gillrey's lips pinched tightly together. "Are you not satisfied with the other gowns I delivered?"

"No, quite the opposite," Rose was quick to assure her, "they are all so lovely, truly they are."

"You simply wish for another one?"

"Precisely. It just occurred to me the other evening that Rose would look quite exceptional in coquelicot. Do you not agree?"

"But of course I do. Do you have a style in mind?"

Both ladies shook their head no. "Very well. Take a look at some fashion plates while I retrieve the fabric."

Directly in front of the shop's window was a dainty table featuring stacks of *La Belle Assemblée*. The women seated themselves on opposite sides of the table and began thumbing through the various plates, remarking on the styles that caught their eye. Rose was particularly fond of the scalloped edged skirts that were the height of fashion at the moment.

"Here we are," Madame Gillrey said behind the bolts of fabric she was balancing in her arms.

The women rose and followed her to the counter where she

deposited several bolts of different fabrics all in shades of red. Rose's hands trailed along the fabric, feeling the varying textures. Madame Gillrey held the bolts, one by one, up to her face, inspecting the shade against her pale skin.

"This one will be perfect," she exclaimed, indicating the lustring.

Adel agreed. "How long will it take?"

This was the moment Rose knew Madame Gillrey would begin her game, insisting she was busy and that it would take a ridiculous amount of time to complete, in hopes that Adel would offer her more money to finish it sooner.

"Normally it would take me a se'enight, but the season is in full swing, and one can hardly expect me to produce a dress of as fine a quality as I am known for in such a short time."

Adel was expert at playing this game. "But the Livingston Ball is a fortnight away; surely you could have it done by then."

Madame Gillrey was thoughtful. "No, my lady, 'tis unfortunate but true, I cannot promise it will be completed by then."

"What if I offer to pay you double your normal fee?"

Rose watched as greed lit up Madame Gillrey's eyes, but the shrewd lady still tried for more. "That is very generous of you, my lady, and I wish I could accept, but I cannot. The Duchess of Chamberly has commissioned another new wardrobe for her daughter, and she insists it be completed before the end of the month. You do understand, don't you?"

Squaring her shoulders, Adel handed the fashion plate she was holding back to Madame Gillrey. "I understand perfectly. It would seem that I am to take my business elsewhere." Adel grabbed Rose's arm and began leading her towards the door.

Normally this kind of encounter would make Rose squirm with discomfort, but she had seen Adel and Madame Gillrey in action before and knew it was all a part of their bargaining game. Truthfully, she couldn't tell who enjoyed these little exchanges more, Adel or Madame Gillrey.

Adel's hand was on the doorknob when Madame Gillrey called out from behind them, "Wait, perhaps we can come to an agreement."

"You have a fortnight to complete the dress at the rate of double your normal fee. If those terms are not agreeable, we will leave now."

"You are a tough woman to bargain with, my lady," she sighed dramatically, though a tiny smile formed on her thin lips. "Alas, I will agree to do it, but only for you. I insist you do not tell your friends of our arrangement, for I would hate to be inundated with ladies insisting I make them new gowns in such a rush and at such a fair price."

Adel smiled, "I will not tell a soul." She reached into her reticule and pulled out some money which she handed to the modiste. "I will pay you half now and the other half upon delivery of the gown."

"You will not be disappointed."

"I am certain I won't be. I look forward to seeing your creation, good day."

As soon as they were free from the shop, Rose looked at Adel and laughed. "Who taught you to do that?"

"Barter with shopkeepers?" she asked.

"Yes, it's really quite impressive. I could never be so bold."

"Unfortunately, I have never had a problem with that. It's a trait that has gotten me into trouble at times, but at other times, such as in there, it has proven quite useful. Look," she exclaimed as she pointed through the carriages parked on the side of the street to the other side, "a woman peddling pineapples. Let's see if we can procure one without draining the coffers."

The idea excited Rose immensely. "Oh, that would be delightful. I have never tasted one, though I have seen them at nearly every party I have attended this season."

"Well, then we shall get one to display at my next dinner party, and before the night is over, we will cut it open and let all sample of its goodness. I tasted it for the first time at the Earl and Countess of Danford's. It's quite exotic. Griffin did not care for it, but I found it quite pleasing."

The women waited until the street was clear before strolling across to the other side. Rose eyed the strange fruit curiously as they approached. There were only a few in the cart, though that wasn't altogether surprising. The climate in Britain was not conducive to growing the exotic fruit. They required special greenhouses called pineries and a lot of attention from skilled gardeners, thus making them an expensive indulgence to produce and even more expensive to acquire. Rose was curious to see if Adel would truly purchase one that day and if so, at what cost.

"Can I interest you in a pineapple, milady? I have a special price just for you."

Rose ignored the exchange as she looked upon the strange fruit, it's textured, prickly skin calling to her fingers to touch it. She reached out to see what it would feel like. Her fingers had barely grazed the skin when the peddler barked, "Do not touch that, milady. That is valuable goods."

Her hand retracted at once as her cheeks turned warm. "I'm sorry," she mumbled as she glanced at the woman and gasped. Holding her hand as if it had been burned, she began backing away from the cart in haste.

A carriage swerved to miss her narrowly, it's driver yelling angrily down at her, but she didn't hear what he was saying. Turning, she began dashing back the way they had come. The only thing she was capable of doing in the moment was fleeing, and flee she did, all the way down Bond Street until she arrived at her brother's carriage and let herself inside before the footman even had time to hop down from his perch.

Chapter Thirteen

Cameron's eyes were burning and dry. He had been pouring over lists and lists of people for hours, trying to determine if there was a common denominator in each murder besides Lord Moncrief, and thus, Lady Rose. He'd had his man of affairs, who was a trusted confidant in his business as secret agent, produce a list of each of the deceased's household staff and family members while he added any close friends that he was aware of to the lists.

It was tedious work sorting through the lists trying to determine if there were any names in common or any possible connections, but he was determined to prove Rose's innocence. He was so determined, in fact, that he had done nothing but work on solving the case since his return from Manhall Manor.

It had been several days since he had seen Rose, and interestingly enough, he found that he missed her and thought of her often.

Stretching out his long legs beneath his desk, he carefully stacked the lists he had been pouring over and slid them into one of the drawers, locking it securely with a tiny brass key he then placed in his fob pocket. It was time he remedied that, for he missed her so.

Within the hour, he found himself sitting in the Straton's drawing room. He had come to call upon Rose, but to his disappointment, it was Lady Straton that greeted him.

"Hello, Lord deCourtenay."

He rose from his seat to greet her. "Good day, Lady Straton. I came to call upon Rose."

"I assumed as much," she said with a smile as she sat in a chair opposite of his and smoothed her skirt across her lap. "Unfortunately, Rose has not been entertaining callers. She had a bit of a...fright several days ago and hasn't quite felt well enough to socialize."

Concern marred his brow. "A fright? Whatever happened?"

"We were out shopping on Bond Street, Rose and me, when she had an encounter with her old ladies maid who now peddles pineapples on the street. It has put her in quite the decline, I'm afraid."

"I don't quite understand."

"Of course you don't, for I haven't done an adequate job of explaining. Shall I ring for tea first?"

"No," he was quick to answer. "I would prefer to hear why this encounter was so upsetting."

"Very well. I normally wouldn't be one to divulge such information to you, but I can sense that you care for Rose and I believe she would tell you herself if she were feeling up to the task. Rose's husband was

not a pleasant man, in fact, I would go so far as to label him evil."
Lady Straton shuddered in disgust. "He was abusive to Rose from the
moment they were wed. Not only did he harm her physically, but he
also kept her in deplorable living conditions while he gambled away
his inheritance and paraded around society with his mistresses. When
I met her, she was being kept in a run-down townhouse with hardly
any belongings, save it be her ladies maid that stayed on, despite the
fact that Lord Moncrief had not been paying her dues. She was the
only friend Rose had."

Though Cameron was aware of some of Rose's past, he had not
been privy to such detail and the thought of the girl being treated so
horribly pierced his heart with sorrow. "Was she not then pleased to
see her former maid?"

"Not in the least. At one time she was Rose's only friend, and that is
what made her betrayal even more painful. Lord Moncrief's gambling
addiction and his subsequent financial ruin were mentioned in the
gossip pages. I don't like to admit this, for it is long buried in my past,
but during my first season I wrote a gossip column under the alias of
Mrs. Tiddlyswan."

Cameron's mouth hung open in shock. "But that column still runs
in the Morning Post."

"Yes," she admitted with a slight roll of her eyes, "though it is not
authored by me, I can assure you. I quit the column and someone,
who I do not know the identity of, took over. Whoever took my place
was the one to write about Lord Moncrief. When the article was
printed, he was furious. He suspected that Rose had something to do

with it so naturally, he went to see her. She assured him she knew nothing about it. Her maid sat by and watched as her husband beat her for knowing the identity of the person who made him out to be a fool but refusing to tell him since, at that point, everyone thought it was me who had written it. She felt betrayed and hurt that her closest friend would not attempt to help her and afterward when she lay bloodied and bruised on the ground, her maid spat upon her and left without saying a word. She has not seen her in years, until the other day on Bond Street, and it was not a pleasant encounter. I have never seen Rose look so frightened."

Cameron could barely contain himself as he listened to Lady Straton recount the horrendous tale. His hands were clenched tightly into fists as his jaw twitched angrily. The thought of anyone harming Rose made him feel murderous. "Who is she? Who is this maid that has hurt and upset her so?"

Before Lady Straton could answer, Lord Straton sauntered into the room. "Darling, whatever are you saying to Lord deCourtenay that has upset him so?"

"I was telling him about Rose's encounter with Esther. He came to call on her, and I needed to explain why she wasn't able to accept his visit," she quickly defended herself.

Lord Straton's face hardened. "I do not think that was necessary information to divulge to merely a suitor."

Cameron prickled at being called "simply a suitor", for, in truth, he was much more. He was tempted to defend himself, to tell them he had been hired by the Main Office and that his goal at this point was to clear her tarnished name, but he couldn't allow his pride to overtake him. Instead, he rose from his chair and turned to Lord Straton, "I can assure you that the information shared today will not be shared with anyone. I appreciate your wife's honesty and it is my fondest hopes that Lady Rose can recover soon."

Before Cameron had a chance to excuse himself, the butler appeared and announced, "You have another visitor, my lord. Shall I send him in?"

"I suppose," Lord Straton sighed wearily.

It took an inordinate amount of self-control for Cameron to remain impassive as Andrew was shown into the room. What he was doing there, he had no idea.

"What can I do for you, sir?" Lord Straton asked curiously.

"I have come to deliver some unfortunate news. The Earl of Westingham is your father, is he not?"

"Unfortunately," Lord Straton mumbled.

Ignoring his comment, Andrew continued, "He has been found dead of an apparent murder."

Lady Straton gasped loudly as she exclaimed, "Somebody has killed him?"

"It would appear to be the case. I was summoned to the scene as part of the Bow Street Runners and can verify that your father indeed was poisoned."

"By who?" Lord Straton asked in shock.

"That has yet to be determined. The butler seems to think that your sister may have had something to do with it. Is she available for questioning?"

"My sister would never do such a thing," Lord Straton roared, offended by the accusation.

"Is she available for questioning?" Andrew asked once more, his voice firm and unyielding.

Cameron stepped forward. "This is preposterous. Lady Rose had nothing to do with her father's death."

Andrew turned and looked at him, "And how can you be certain?"

"Because I was with her."

"Interesting. It would appear that I need to question you as well."

"I will answer anything you wish if we can speak alone." Turning to Lord and Lady Straton, he instructed, "Go fetch Rose while I talk with this man alone. We will settle this nonsense right away."

When they were finally alone, Cameron turned to Andrew and hissed, "What are you doing?"

"Investigating a murder. I find it quite interesting that Lady Rose is the prime suspect in yet another one."

"She didn't do it," he stated forcefully.

"Just like she didn't kill all those other men either? Look, Cameron, I'm not entirely sure what is going on with you and the girl, but it has rendered you useless. You have yet to provide any information that will either incriminate her or pardon her, yet people all around her keep ending up dead. I regret to inform you that you have been dismissed from the case. Your aid is no longer needed."

Cameron felt as if he had been issued a blow. His stomach clenched in dread, for he knew that he had to help her. "I promise you that I will figure this out. You haven't given me enough time."

"You've had ample of time, but instead of using it to look at the obvious, you have been wasting it trying to find reasons to convince yourself the lady is innocent. You've allowed your heart to distract you from the truth."

"My heart isn't involved," he seethed.

"No?" Andrew asked, one eyebrow raised skeptically. "Then you're merely a fool."

Cameron was about to plant him a facer when Lord Straton, Lady Straton, and Rose entered the room. His eyes went to Rose at once—she looked awful. Her face looked sallow and her dark eyes sunken while her raven hair hung limply down her back. He wanted to go to her and offer her some assurance, but he forced himself to remain where he was.

"Lady Rose, forgive me, but I must ask you some questions." Rose nodded solemnly as she remained standing. "On the night of Thursday last, where were you?"

"I had gone to visit my father at Manhall Manor."

"And for what intent was your visit?"

"I had been summoned by him. He informed me in a missive that he was dying and that he wished for me to come."

Lord Straton interjected hopefully, "Yes, my father informed us he was dying. Are you quite certain his death wasn't a result of natural causes?"

"Quite," Andrew replied impatiently before resuming his questioning of Rose. "How long were you at Manhall Manor?"

"Only for the evening. I had intended on staying longer but..." her sentence trailed off as her eyes flickered to Cameron's.

"But what?"

"I had an argument with my father and he commanded me to leave."

"What was this argument about?"

Rose sighed. "About his failure to be a loving father, about things he had done that had caused a lot of hurt to my brother and me."

"What sort of things?"

"Mostly the fact that he forced me to wed the Baron Moncrief."

"Did you hate him for that?"

Rose was slower to answer this question than she had been the others, but she eventually muttered a quiet, "Yes."

"Enough for you to kill him?"

Everyone in the room but Andrew gasped.

"No," Rose shouted resolutely. "The thought never even occurred to me."

Ignoring her anguished insistence, he asked, "Were you ever alone with your father?"

Rose had to think for a moment, "Yes, but only just briefly."

"Is that when you fed your father the poison that would end his life?"

"No!" she shouted.

Lord Straton stepped forward, placing his body protectively in front of Rose's. "This is the inside of enough. You are questioning her as if she has already been found guilty. She said that she did not kill him, can't you believe her?"

Meanwhile, Cameron's mind had been racing. "Sir, I can understand your reason for suspicion, but please allow me to point something out. Lady Rose was left alone with her father for a brief time. This was when their argument ensued. At the conclusion of the argument, her father banished her from his home and his life, though he told her she could stay the night before traveling back to London. Like it was mentioned previously, I was at Manhall Manor and spoke with Lady Rose immediately following the argument. I told her that she would not be required to stay another moment under her father's roof and that I would bring her back to London at once. She was most eager to leave, as was I. I gathered her trunk from her bedchamber, and we made to leave."

"This is all very fascinating, but does it have a point?"

"Yes, it does. As we were leaving, we had another encounter with her father. He came to the door of his bedchamber, and another conversation ensued. We left promptly after that and returned to London at once. This is my point—if Lady Rose had indeed poisoned her father during the brief period that they were alone, he would have been dead within minutes. Seeing as how she did not, in fact, poison him, he was very much alive and able to walk to his doorway and engage in further conversation later that evening. I can vouch that she left immediately following this final conversation and thus never had a chance to be alone with him again. There is no way she could have done it."

Andrew's face remained stoic. "How can I verify that your story is accurate, that you were truthfully at Manhall Manor and have not concocted a story merely to appease me and acquit Lady Rose?"

Lord Straton stepped forward. "I can verify it is true. Lord deCourtenay's carriage showed up at my house in the early morning hours. He had indeed escorted Rose home, even carried her sleeping form inside."

Andrew was thoughtful for several long minutes before taking the small pad of paper he had been writing notes on and stuffing it into his jacket pocket. "Very well. It would appear that my work here is done."

Cameron watched the butler show Andrew out as he exhaled in relief. One crisis had been averted, but he knew there was still more to come. For though Andrew may have been convinced of Rose's innocence in regards to her father's death, he knew that he wasn't convinced she was innocent of the others.

Chapter Fourteen

Cameron was the first to speak as soon as Andrew left, "I'm grateful that I was here. I can't even imagine what would have happened had I not been able to vouch for Rose."

"Thank you," Lord Straton stated sincerely.

"This entire situation is just awful," Rose cried. "I may very well end up hanged for crimes I didn't even commit. Perhaps I should have killed my husband all those years ago, at least then the suspicion would be warranted."

Forgetting for a moment that they weren't alone, Cameron went to Rose and reached for her hands. Holding tightly, he looked deep into the black recesses of her eyes and said lowly, "Don't say that. I can assure you this will all get straightened out."

"But if it doesn't?"

"Then I will kill Esther with my bare hands, and we can go to the gallows together."

"Who told you about Esther?"

Lady Straton blushed guiltily. "It was me."

Rose looked back to him. "Why would you kill her?"

"Because of what she did to you, and so that we wouldn't have to be separated."

Behind them, Lord Straton cleared his throat loudly. "Are you making an offer for my sister?"

Cameron gave her an adorable, lopsided grin. "Yes, I am. If she will have me, that is."

Rose sucked in her cheek and bit down as she thought. Was this all a part of their ploy? Things kept getting stranger and stranger, and she wasn't certain what was reality anymore. "You can't marry someone who is suspected of murder," she finally answered.

"Rose," Griffin interjected sharply, "you are not suspected of murder any longer."

Rose realized her mistake. "But someone poisoned father. There's a murderer out there, and we must find out who did it."

"We will not be doing anything," he said a bit forcefully. "I will hire someone to investigate if this Andrew fellow isn't going to continue to do so. In the meantime, I will need to make arrangements for father's funeral."

"Do I have to go?" Rose asked her brother.

"Not if you don't want to. I can go to Manhall Manor by myself."

"I will go with you," Adel said softly before ushering her husband from the room, leaving Cameron and Rose alone, though, for proprieties sake, the door was left propped open.

Rose turned to Cameron and whispered, "You did not have to offer for me like that. I am afraid this scheme is going to be too complicated to unravel when everything else gets straightened out."

He reached up and cupped her cheek in his palm. "I wasn't playacting, Rose. I truly do wish to wed you."

She looked at him strangely, her mouth agape. "I don't understand. I am a woman who is suspected of murder. I have nothing good to offer you. If you marry me, you may never have any posterity. And if —"

Cameron silenced her with a laugh. "Are you trying to persuade me from my cause? I am aware of all those things you mentioned and I still very much wish to wed you. Rose," he breathed longingly, "I do not give a fig about any of that. Please consent to become my wife."

When that intense stare of his settled upon her, Rose shivered. How could she deny this man anything when he looked at her so? She truly never believed she'd ever wed again, yet here, standing before her, was a charming man who wished to become her husband and not because he sought to gain anything from the union. In fact, the way she saw it, the union would be nothing but a disadvantage to him. Yet despite all of that, he still wanted her.

When she hesitated to give him an answer, he continued, "Rose, I promise you that I can keep you safe, that I will discover who is framing you for these murders, for certainly, that is what is going on. I vow to protect you at whatever cost."

Rose instantly thought of her dreams involving him and realized that perhaps they had been a bit prophetic. But promises of protection were not enough to warrant their marriage. "And what of love, Cameron? Is ours to be a union completely devoid of the emotion?"

"Do you love me?" he asked frankly.

She was thoughtful for a moment and decided, to be honest with him. "I'm not entirely certain I know how to love anyone, besides my family that is. Isn't that sad?"

"Yes," he admitted as he brushed a stray tear away with his thumb, "but that is due to no shortcoming of yours. You do don't know how to love because no one has shown you how. I could do that if you'd let me."

She swallowed past the lump forming in her throat. "You'd do that for me?"

"Of course," he said as he nodded fervently. "I'm not an expert in the emotion, for I haven't ever been in love before, but there are a few things I can surmise. For starters, I think it would be hard to love someone who made you scared and threatened your safety. I can promise I will never lay a hand on you in anger. I also think it would be exceptionally hard to love someone who didn't genuinely care about you and show you that they did. I care about you, Rose, very deeply. I care about the pain you have hidden in your heart. I can see by the shadows in your eyes that you haven't been able to free yourself entirely from the pain, though I know you have tried valiantly to do so. I care about the fact that you love that blasted dog I bequeathed to you with an intensity that makes me jealous," Rose couldn't help but laugh a bit. Cameron smiled then continued, "I care about the perfume that you use, for it drives me mad with distraction."

To prove his point, he leaned down and stuck his head into the crook of her neck and inhaled deeply. She felt his warm breath slither across her skin as he slowly exhaled and muttered, "Delicious. Do you know what else I care about, Rose?"

His eyes had returned to hers as she answered with a small, "No."

"I care about your dreams and your passions. What is it that you dream about at night when the day's worries are behind you? What is it that you want more than anything?"

"You," she admitted almost shyly.

Cameron scooped her into his arms, his lips crushing into her own. His warm, pliable lips intertwined with hers in a lovers' dance. She kissed him with a passion reserved just for him as her spirit soared, a broken part of her set free. He tasted of all her hidden hopes, of all her buried dreams and his touch spoke of tenderness.

Pulling back, he leaned his forehead against her own. "But do you think you could learn to love me?"

She silently searched her soul as she pondered his question, wanting to give him a truthful answer. "I believe with your excellent teaching I could."

"I promise you that I will never stop trying to earn your affection. Ours will not be a union of misery as you have previously known."

"I believe you," she muttered with genuine confidence.

Giving her a hesitant, yet hopeful smile he asked, "Does that mean you will consent to become my wife?"

"Yes."

Cameron threw his arms around her waist and lifted her feet off the ground, spinning her in a circle as they both laughed.

Their celebrations were cut short by Griffin's return to the room. "I surmise you two have agreed to wed, to which I give my hearty consent, by the way," he said while speaking directly to Cameron. "Unfortunately, the wedding will have to be delayed for a spell. It is only proper that we spend the next several months in mourning, if only as a display of propriety, for we all know that none of us is truly saddened by father's death. I'm afraid you won't be able to participate in the remainder of the season. Adel and I have decided that it will be best if you retire to Manhall Manor with us. I can spend the upcoming months sorting through the estate's affairs while you observe your mourning. As soon as the proper time has passed, you two can be wed."

Rose knew that her brother was right, but the thought of quitting the season and leaving Cameron behind in Town was depressing.

"I have sent your maid to your bedchamber to begin packing your trunk. I suggest you go meet her so you can instruct her sufficiently. You will have time to say your goodbyes before we depart."

"Very well," she spoke with a touch of reluctance before doing as he instructed.

Though none of them were truly mourning the loss of the late Earl of Westingham, the house had taken on a somber air. Rose found her maid working quietly yet swiftly as she entered her bedchamber, folding her belongings neatly before packing them into her trunk.

She went to her dressing room and began assisting when her maid stopped her. "My lady, you do not have to do that. Take a seat next to the hearth while I finish up. I won't be much longer; then I can help you change your clothing."

When her maid produced her black crepe travel dress, Rose nearly burst into tears. Her maid laid the dress on the bed and came to her, wrapping her in her embrace. "My lady, I'm truly sorry for your loss."

Rose managed a small laugh as she pulled back and wiped at her eyes. "I'm not crying over Father if you can believe it. The tears I am shedding are on my mother's behalf. That dress," she said as she motioned towards the bed, "is one that I wore during my mourning after her death. Seeing it again has brought all those painful emotions to the surface. I loved my mother dearly, as did my brother, and her death not only crushed our hearts but it signified the end of my life as I had known it. As soon as my mourning period had passed, I was forced to wed the Baron Moncrief."

Her maid gave her a reassuring squeeze of her hand. "Yes, I should have been sensitive to the painful feelings it would produce, but I had no other option—it is the only proper mourning gown that you have."

"I know, and it's not your fault, truly it isn't. One of these days I hope not to be such an emotional wreck, crying over the slightest things that produce painful memories."

With that being said, Rose allowed her maid to dress her in the gown. She was surprised it still fit nearly as well as it had all those years ago. As soon as she was certain that all of her necessary belongings had been packed, she turned and motioned for Prince to join her at her side. Her hand wound in his thick fur, feeling grateful that at least he would be going to Manhall Manor with her, a piece of Cameron that would be with her during their separation.

"Come on, boy, let's go bid goodbye to Cameron."

Rose smiled as she entered the drawing room and saw Cameron waiting patiently on the settee, one booted foot propped up on his thigh. "I'm sorry it took so long," she said, suddenly feeling shy.

Cameron rose and came to her. "I wouldn't have left before bidding you goodbye and giving you this."

He held up his hand and turned his palm over. Rose watched as a thin, golden chain slid from his grasp and reached up to catch it before it could fall. The weight of the chain, with it's attached charm surprised her. Opening her palm, she beheld a heart-shaped locket engraved with the letter R framed by dainty vines.

Touched by the gesture, her eyes went to his face and found that he was gazing at her intently. "I bought it for you the day I disposed of the other necklace."

He reached for it and told her to turn around so he could clasp it into place around her slender neck. It felt warm against her collarbone, the unfamiliar weight of the locket feeling oddly comforting. She reached up and touched it once more.

"I dread our separation, but know that I will be doing everything I can to solve the case. My greatest joy lies in the fact that our time apart will be followed by the happiest of occasions." He bent and placed a feather-soft kiss on the back of her neck, "I wait longingly for the day you will become mine."

"I pray the time goes swiftly," she admitted, dreading the

separation already though it had yet to begin.

It wasn't until she was alone in the carriage with Prince, awaiting her maid to join them for the trip to Manhall Manor that she thought to open the locket. Pressing the clasp that held it together, it popped open, and a small folded square of parchment fell into her lap. She removed her gloves and set them on the bench next to her so she could unfold the tightly folded paper. She had to squint to read the tiny, meticulous writing:

> *If I could give you anything,*
> *I'd give you wings so you could fly.*
> *I'd bandage up your wounded heart,*
> *and hold you while you cry.*
> *If I could give you anything,*
> *a lifetime of endless love it would be,*
> *a journey filled with happiness,*
> *together, you and me.*

Chapter Fifteen

So much had occurred in the first few days of being back at Manhall Manor. Griffin had met with the funeral furnisher to make preparations for their father's funeral. They had hired two women to come in and wash and dress his body in preparation since neither of them had wanted to do it. Griffin insisted that the funeral be kept small, though the furnisher kept trying to insist that the Earl of Westingham deserved a fancy affair. Both Griffin and Rose had no desire to give him any more than what he had given their mother, by way of a funeral. The gathering would be small, the service brief.

Having Adel and her three boys present at the manor helped alleviate some of the darkness that enshrouded the place. Having the halls filled with laughter and the noise of the rambunctious trio helped turn the residence from a mausoleum of despair into something that resembled an actual home.

Rose was in the nursery, reading stories to Henry and Conrad while Adel fed Damien when Griffin walked in, unannounced, the black armband of mourning tied around his arm standing out in stark contrast next to his white shirtsleeves. "Rose, Father's lawyer has arrived and is requesting our presence in the study."

Rose closed the book she had been reading to the children and stood. "I'm not sure why I'm suddenly nervous," she admitted frankly.

"I'm a bit nervous myself."

"Do you wish for me to come too?" Adel asked from her position in the rocking chair.

Griffin looked down at her and their son, and his face softened. "No, Damien will be mad if I force you to cut his meal short. I will bring you word as soon as the meeting is through."

Adel nodded then Griffin and Rose left the nursery to meet the lawyer in the study. Rose was not at all surprised to meet her father's lawyer and find him to be cold and aloof. She was certain that no one that worked for her father could be even remotely likable.

Griffin instructed them all to sit before offering the man a drink, to which he declined.

"The late Earl of Westingham told me to deliver these missives to you upon his death. As soon as I heard word, I arranged to have them delivered." He leaned across the desk and handed two envelopes to Griffin, which he hesitantly took. "I am also instructed to read his will, though you shouldn't find any surprises there. His title and his estate all rightfully belong to you, as his heir, and the few belongings he held outside of that are divided equitably between you both."

"Very good. Let us do the formal reading then so that we can be done with it."

The lawyer nodded as he produced the document from his case and proceeded to read the short will. Just like he had said, there were no surprises, which kind of surprised Rose, for she had almost expected him to do something vindictive just to hurt her or Griffin, or both.

Griffin wasted no time seeing that the lawyer was shown out as soon as the formalities had taken place. He turned to Rose and handed her the letter marked with her name and admitted, "I'm dreading reading this," as he held his own missive up before him.

"I don't find myself anxious either. Part of me wants to throw it into the fire, unread. It can't hold anything pleasant, can it?"

"There's only one way to find out." Griffin pried the seal open and began reading his letter at once. She watched him, trying to read his expression, but it was unreadable.

Her hands were shaking as she unfolded the parchment and stared down upon her father's familiar writing. Her eyes refused to focus for a moment, as unwilling as her heart to hear what he had to say. Finally, she forced them to concentrate on the words written on the page and she read:

Rose,

My life is coming to an end, and I know I can't possibly expect to go to a place of peace while my conscience is weighed down with guilt. I don't have the energy to write to you and explain why I am the way that I am, suffice it to say that my life has been filled with deep regrets and it has hardened me

*into a man my own mother would not recognize were she still
alive.*

*I have made many mistakes on your behalf, the worst of which
was forcing you to wed the Baron Moncrief. I never told you at
the time, but General Howe was eager to offer for you and in
my fear of the man I was quick to pawn you off on Lord
Moncrief instead, hoping that it would be a better, safer union
than the one I foresaw with the General. I later learned just
how wrong that decision was. My actions not only ruined your
life, but they also destroyed any hope I had of an improved
relationship with Griffin as well.*

*I've never known how to make this right with you. I couldn't
save you from your marriage, even if I had wanted to. You
were no longer my property but belonged to your husband
instead. I am not a man of great emotion and was never able
to bring myself to apologize to you in person. I summoned you
home in the hopes that you would find it in your heart to care
for me while I found it in my heart to apologize. I regret
deeply that isn't what occurred. I hope in time you can find it
in your heart to forgive me for my actions, though I wouldn't
blame you if you couldn't. And despite contrary belief, I love
you, Rose, I always have.*
Your Father

Silent tears were streaming down Rose's face by the time she finished the letter. Oh, how different life would have been had her father showed even a portion of the emotion and concern he had just expressed in his letter. Pain and heartache that left permanent scars upon her body and heart could have been largely avoided. Their family could have been preserved instead of divided by bitterness.

She looked to Griffin, and for the first time in their adult life, she saw tears pooled in his dark eyes as well. "Why couldn't he have said those things to us while he was living?"

"Because I wouldn't have listened," he stated honestly.

Rose thought back to their last visit, and she knew it was true for her as well. Her heart had been so hardened towards her father, she didn't want to hear what he may have said. Part of her wished she would have been more pleasant and agreed to do as he asked instead of provoking his anger. Maybe then she would have gotten the apology she had craved so long.

"Perhaps if I would have stayed when he called for me instead of arguing with him, he'd still be alive," she voiced her thoughts aloud. "I could have kept him safe."

"Or ended up dead yourself. I have a feeling I might know who killed father."

"Who?"

"I'm not going to say until I know if it's true or not. I would hate to tarnish a person's good name if I was wrong."

"And how do you expect to find out if your suspicion is correct?"

"It would appear I will need to do a bit of investigating myself. As soon as father is buried, I will be returning to London."

"Can't you just call Andrew and have him investigate? I don't like the thought of you putting yourself in harm's way."

"If it's who I suspect it is, I'm not about to let anyone know of my suspicions. I would not want to be wrong on this."

Trying another tactic to keep him from going, she said, "Adel is not going to want you to go."

His shoulders drooped a bit. "Yes, I know that she won't. Perhaps we can keep my true purpose for returning to London a secret."

"You've never lied to her before."

"It wouldn't be a lie," he barked irritably. "I would only withhold a portion of the truth."

Rose's brows arched with a hint of amusement. "Like the time you withheld the fact that your pursuit of her was due to a lost bet? You didn't precisely lie to her then either, just withheld the truth."

"Blast it all, Rose; this is different. I will tell her that I have to return to take care of some business relating to father's death, which is true. I will simply wait to explain the rest until I know if it is true or not. You must give me your word that you will not tell her my true reasons for going and give her cause to worry. We suspect she is with child. She does not need to worry right now."

"Truly?" Rose asked excitedly, focusing on his good news instead of all the rest.

"Yes, though it's too early to know for certain. Please, just trust me on this."

Nodding her head she reluctantly agreed. "I will do what you ask, but I don't like it."

"I know you don't," he said gently, "but telling Adel the true purpose of my trip will not help either of us."

"But Griffin, I don't want any harm to befall you." Her eyes searched her brother's, and her heart swelled with love. He had always been so good to her, and he was the only family she had left. "Your family needs you, we all do."

Her tall brother came to her, wrapping her in his embrace. "I won't do anything foolish, I promise you."

Rose snorted, "So many promises I am not certain you can keep."

"I'm wounded to hear that you have such little faith in me, dear sister."

"I'm just scared," she admitted honestly.

"You don't need to be. Everything will turn out just fine. I will go to London and take care of things as promptly as possible and return home to take care of everything here. It will be so swift; you will hardly have time to notice my absence before I return once more. And," he continued, "if you are a good girl, I will bring you a treat."

Rose couldn't help but laugh at him. "You make me feel like a child saying things like that."

"You are a child," he joked.

"Hardly," she said with a roll of her eyes. "Now tell me what you will bring me if I behave."

"I don't think I should tell you. It'll mean more to you if I keep you in suspense."

She pulled from his arms, giving him a stern look as she stomped one foot on the ground. "I hate surprises; you know that. Tell me or I'll..."

"Throw a tantrum reminiscent of the ones you used to throw when you were indeed a child?"

"If I do will you tell me?"

Griffin smiled. "Why don't you try it and find out."

"Just tell me," she whined, hating the way he teased her at times, though truthfully she was grateful for the distraction.

He tweaked her nose and chuckled, "If you promise to be a good girl and help Adel with the boys while I am gone, I will see what I can do about arranging a visit from Lord deCourtenay."

"I would love that," she squealed, "though I am uncertain he can get away right now."

Griffin looked at her strangely, "I am certain there aren't any entertainments of the season so pressing they would keep him from his affianced."

Yes, that was true she thought, but she knew he was busy trying to find the murderer before time ran out. Oh, how she wished she would get word from him saying he had solved things. But now, she would not only be worrying about him, but she'd also be worrying about Griffin as well, and the thought was almost too much to bear.

Collapsing into the chair, she let her head fall into her hands as she muttered, "Why can't life be simple and serene?"

Griffin, looking very much the part of the worried older brother, knelt beside her and asked, "Are things not well between you and Lord deCourtenay?"

"It's not that, I'm just worried I suppose. I don't like being suspected of murder, I don't like being separated from Cameron and having to wait to wed him until I come out of mourning, and I don't like having to keep secrets from Adel."

"Rose, you were suspected of murder for the briefest of moments. You can lay that worry to rest already. As far as the everything else, there is nothing to be done for it right now. I can understand your concern, for your life has not been easy, but things are good now, better than they've ever been actually. You can stop looking for things to go wrong and start expecting them to go right."

Rose took his words to heart, but as the next few days progressed, the feeling that he was wrong kept encroaching upon the peace she fought so hard to feel.

They buried their father in the cemetery next to their mother on a day that was rainy and bleak. It seemed fitting to Rose, for even though he had left her an apology letter, her memories of her father would probably always remain somewhat dark.

She wasn't sure if it was the somberness of the occasion that caused an unnerving feeling to settle in her stomach, or if it was Griffin's impending departure. Either way, she was convinced that something bad was about to happen and she didn't like the feeling one bit.

Chapter Sixteen

Holding a brandy in his hand, Cameron swirled the amber liquid around and around as he stared across his table at White's, not looking at anything in particular. Though Andrew had informed him that he had been removed from the case, nothing was preventing him from trying to solve it. He had decided to go about his business as he had before, except this time he felt a greater urgency, for he was nearly desperate to prove Rose's innocence. If there was one more murder that pointed to her in any way, he was certain the Main Office wouldn't hesitate to convict her.

He had used his contacts to get into every one of the deceased's households, using hired help to go undercover to question the servants, but he had yet to find a common link or anything out of the ordinary, and it was frustrating him greatly.

"Care for some more brandy, my lord?"

Cameron snapped out of his reverie and glanced to the attendant standing at his table. "No, thank you."

He downed the last bit of brandy in his glass then stood to leave when he glanced across the room and noticed Lord Straton sitting at a table with his good friend, the Earl of Danford. He had to do a double-take to make sure it truly was him, but sure enough, it was. Filled with curiosity, he sauntered over to the table to say hello.

"Good evening, gentleman."

Both men looked up at him, welcoming smiles displayed on their faces. "Lord deCourtenay, have a seat," Lord Straton offered as he signaled the attendant to bring him a drink.

Cameron sat, ignoring the freshly produced glass of brandy, knowing it wouldn't be wise for him to imbibe. "May I be so bold to ask you what you are doing in Town? I hadn't expected to see you for quite some time."

"Yes, I hadn't anticipated returning so soon, but I felt a degree of urgency."

Both men looked at Lord Straton curiously before Cameron asked, "Is everything well with your family?" Fear gripped his heart as he waited for a response. He wasn't sure what he would do if Lord Straton told him that something had happened to Rose.

He reached into his jacket pocket and produced a folded up piece of parchment and breathed deeply as if he was expecting the breath to fortify him for what he was about to say. "My father wrote me a letter before he died and I must admit that some of what he revealed was quite shocking to me."

"Your father was a miserable man," Lord Danford interjected. "You cannot allow his pathetic deathbed ramblings to affect you."

"I cannot argue that point, but his letter actually proved to be quite the revelation. Can I trust you both to keep what I'm about to share with you an absolute secret? I have a strong suspicion I know who may have killed my father, and I have returned to London to do some investigating of my own."

Cameron's inner agent perked up at his admission. "Of course you can trust me to keep it a secret."

"You know I won't utter a word of it to anyone," Lord Danford added his assurance as well.

Lord Straton leaned in close, prompting the other men to do so as well. With all three of their heads nearly touching, he started speaking softly, "My father informed me that the reason he forced Rose to wed the Baron Moncrief was to keep her safe, ironically enough. Apparently, my mother's cousin had set his cap for her, but my mother refused to allow his pursuit for she knew of his true character. He was a violent, spoiled child who had been accused of taking whatever he wanted from whoever he wanted, using force to get his way. My mother learned of this behavior firsthand when she witnessed him forcing himself upon a chambermaid. Needless to say, she wasn't able to stop him, and he ended up threatening her with her life if she told anyone about what he had done."

"Deplorable human being," Lord Danford spat. "Though I'm not sure Lord Moncrief was any better."

"Pathetic, isn't it? It seems that Rose was destined to marry a vile cad. As you can imagine, my mother's cousin was not pleased at all when my parents refused his offer."

"But do you think he killed your father for something that happened years ago?" Lord Danford asked a bit skeptically.

"There's more. My father seemed to suspect that Mother's cousin was the one who spooked her horse the morning she died. Benedict, you know she was a very accomplished horsewoman and the accident was such a shock to all of us. My father was never convinced it was an accident, however. At her funeral, her cousin offered for Rose again and my father, once more, refused him. He married her off to Lord Moncrief, foolishly believing it would be a better union. He was too worried about what my mother's cousin would do to Rose if he didn't get her away from Manhall Manor."

"So you think this cousin was the one who poisoned your father?" Cameron asked.

"Yes, I do. In this letter," he held it between them as he spoke, "my father expressed grave concern on Rose's behalf. He worried that her re-entrance into society would prompt this man to come for her again and he begged me to keep her safe."

"Who is he?"

Lord Straton's head popped up as he gave a cursory glance around the room, making sure no one was paying them any mind before hissing lowly, "General Howe."

Cameron sucked in a startled breath.

"See why I can't just accuse him without proof? No one would believe my word against his. I need proof, hard evidence that it was he who killed my father. I will never be able to prove he was behind my mother's death, but I will not let him get away with murder this time."

Cameron's mind was racing. General Howe was on the list of potential victim's, being one who had won a significant amount of money from Lord Moncrief. He had thought it a bit odd that other men had been killed while he remained untouched, but he was convinced it was due to his increased protection. He closed his eyes and mentally recalled the list of potential victims. The only two still alive were General Howe and Lord Wrencher.

"How do you expect to find out if it was him?" Lord Danford asked.

"Leave it up to me," Cameron blurted.

Both men turned to look strangely at Cameron. "Why would I do that?"

"Because I have connections you do not. Think about it, if General Howe is indeed your father's murderer, it will look highly obvious that you were on to him when you start questioning people and prying into his affairs. I can do the same thing without rousing suspicion."

Lord Straton was thoughtful for a moment. "I see your point. But what can I do? I refuse to return to Manhall Manor until this is figured out."

"The best thing you can do is return home and keep Rose safe while I see to things here. If your suspicions are correct, he may think to harm her next."

Lord Straton's face looked ashen. "I've been a fool not to think of that." Rising, he stuffed the letter back into his jacket pocket and said, "Gentlemen, I must leave at once. Please keep me informed of your findings. A visit to Manhall Manor would be most welcome once you have finished your work here."

"I would like that. I will personally bring word as soon as I learn of anything." Cameron watched Lord Straton leave before turning to Lord Danford. "Can I enlist you to help me?"

"Of course."

Heads bent close together, Cameron informed him of his work as a secret agent. "The Main Office suspects that Rose may be behind the deaths of many prominent men who had won a significant amount of money from her late husband, leaving her penniless upon his death. They suspect her motives are revenge."

"That is absurd," he scoffed. "Rose would never harm a soul."

"I know that as well as you, but they need evidence that it isn't her. So far, I have been unable to provide any. Knowing what we know now, I suspect that perhaps General Howe is behind the murders of these men, and not just the Earl of Westingham's murder."

"I understand why he would kill the earl, but why would he kill those other men?"

"To frame Rose, perhaps."

"If that is the case, he is truly an evil man."

"I will not argue with you there. I'm afraid if I start prying into his affairs, they will suspect me of knowing the truth. We have to get the information we seek without drawing suspicion. This is where you come in. I need you to discover if the General was in London the night the earl was murdered."

"And if he wasn't, I'm certain he has gone to great lengths to hide the fact."

"Yes, but someone in his household would know of his whereabouts. Question the stablehands, the servants, anyone you can think of until you find the information we seek. But I warn you; you must be discreet."

"Of course. I will hopefully have word for you soon. Where should I send it when I do?"

"Do not send anything, come tell me in person. I am staying at my townhouse in Mayfair. You can find me there."

They rose in unison, both men feeling a raw excitement at the prospect of bringing a murderer to justice and freeing Rose from suspicion. Cameron was good at reading people, and his gut instinct told him that Lord Danford could be trusted. He was certain they were going to make a good team.

***

"Jonathan, you have been my valet for a long time, and I feel as if I can trust you," Benedict, the Earl of Danford, spoke lowly to the older gentleman as his aging but agile hands worked swiftly to untie his cravat.

One graying eyebrow arched ever so slightly before he muttered, "Of course, my lord."

"I have some undercover work I need performed, and it's not something I can see to myself."

"What are you up to, my lord?"

"I have been asked to help a friend working for the Main Office solve a murder. I need someone to go to General Howe's residence undercover to discover his whereabouts on the night of Lord Straton's father's death."

Benedict was a bit surprised when Jonathan allowed his normally stoic demeanor to register shock. "General Howe killed the Earl of Westingham?"

"Shhhh," he hissed, glancing to the dressing room door that led into his wife's bedchamber. He knew she would be waiting for him and he didn't want her to overhear any of the conversation. "We do not know if that is the case, though we are urgently trying to find out. My job is to discover where the General was the night the murder occurred."

"With all due respect, my lord, I am much too old to go undercover. Not to mention the fact that I would easily be recognized as your valet."

Benedict grinned, "I wasn't suggesting you go, old man, I was thinking of assigning your son to the task." Jonathan's son, John, worked in the stables as a groom. "If he is successful at getting the information I seek, I will promote him to coachman."

He knew he had gained Jonathan's full attention when the man quickly said, "Yes, shall we send for him now?"

"No, for I am certain Lady Danford is growing impatient waiting for me. Help me into my banyan." Jonathan did as his master instructed. When he was finished, Benedict turned to him, placing one hand on his shoulder and looking him squarely in the eyes, "I will entrust you with the task of informing your son of his assignment. He must be sworn to secrecy, and he must promise me he can be discreet. If he can do that, as well as find out the General's whereabouts the night of the murder, I will reward him greatly. If he fails, however..." Benedict let his sentence trail off ominously.

"You can count on John, my lord, or my name isn't Jonathan Fredrick Winston the Third."

Chapter Seventeen

Cameron was growing impatient. He hadn't heard a single word from Lord Danford for nearly three days now, and he was beginning to wonder if he had decided not to help him. He was about to send for his coach and instruct his driver to take him to the Earl's townhouse when his butler intruded upon his thoughts. "My lord, the Earl of Danford wishes to speak with you."

Cameron rose swiftly, a smile forming on his lips. "What perfect timing. Let him in."

As soon as the door shut tightly behind them, a self-satisfied smile spread across the Earl's face, causing Cameron to feel hopeful. "Can I offer you a drink?"

"Take a seat," the earl commanded. "You and I both know that I'm not here to be entertained."

Though it was his home and he was usually the one to do all the commanding, Cameron did as the earl bade. Intertwining his fingers together, he leaned across his desk and asked hopefully, "Did you find out where the General was on the night of the murder?"

"I did, and I must take a minute to gloat about the genius servant who acquired the information. My valet's son, John, took one of my finest horses to the General's stables. He informed the lead groom that General Howe had summoned him there the week prior so he could inspect the horse, with the intent of purchasing it if he was satisfied. John expressed great disappointment at the fact that the General did not keep their appointment. It was his idea to go in there and pretend as if he already knew the General wasn't in Town that day. He figured they would either deny his claims or be quick to confirm them."

"And which was it?"

"The latter. Apparently, the General has a sizable pinerie at his estate in Bedfordshire that produces quite an impressive income for the man. He had gone to check on it and see that everything was running smoothly."

Before he fully let disappointment overcome him, Cameron had to ask, "You are certain that is where he was? Or are his servants simply trying to cover for him?"

"John felt quite confident that they were speaking the truth."

"Fiend seize it, that was not the information I was hoping to gain."

"I know it wasn't, but at least you can scratch General Howe off of your list of suspects."

"He was the only one on my list," Cameron growled irritably. "Where do I go from here?"

Lord Danford shrugged his broad shoulders, "You're the secret agent, not me. You'll figure it out."

The problem was, Cameron wasn't certain that he would. His mind was racing as he withdrew inside of himself, nearly forgetting that Lord Danford was present until he heard him clear his throat loudly. "If that is all, I best be getting on my way."

"Not so fast. Sit," he ordered and watched as the earl did so, his face unreadable. "Before I can confidently scratch General Howe off my list, I wish to visit Bedfordshire and see if he truly was in residence the night of the murder, as his servants claim."

"Then, by all means, go there and ask."

"You know I can't do that, for the same reason I couldn't show up at his townhouse asking questions about his whereabouts."

"Well, what do you expect me to do? Send John there with my horse?"

"That might appear fishy. Do you trust your man of affairs?"

"With my life," Lord Danford said confidently.

"Good. Send him to Bedfordshire to investigate under the guise that you are looking to start a pinerie yourself."

Cameron could see the wheels spinning in the earl's head. "Yes, I think that could work."

"It will work," he said with conviction.

The next quarter of an hour was spent going over things, making sure their plan was foolproof. By the time Lord Danford had left, Cameron was feeling confident that soon they would know for certain whether General Howe was their man or not. He was grateful that

Lord Danford was so willing to help him acquire the information he needed.

Propping his booted feet up on his desk, he placed his hands behind his head and stared up at the coffered ceiling. Oh, how he wished this whole mess was straightened out and that Rose's mourning period was over so he could wed her and begin showing her how she deserved to be treated. Though she had only been gone from London for a sen'night, it felt like longer than that, and he missed her terribly.

His mind quickly estimated how long it would take Lord Danford's man of affairs to accomplish his task—two days travel to Bedfordshire, at least a day, if not two spent acquiring the information, and another two days travel back to London. Plenty of time to see Rose.

His feet returned to the floor as his spirits soared. He would await word from Lord Danford that their plan had been set into motion, then he would arrange the visit. Being in her presence was just the thing he needed.

***

"I am surprised at the amount of things your father has held onto all of these years," Adel said in disgust as she threw another outdated dress coat onto the growing pile in the center of the floor. "Too bad you didn't pilfer some of this stuff for Benedict to wear when you concocted that silly bet. If you had, I'm certain you would have proven victorious."

Adel was referring to the time Griffin and his friends had convinced Lord Danford to dress as an unfashionable halfwit for the season

162

while attempting to woo a diamond of the first water, the Duke of Chesley's eldest daughter, Lady Gillian. Apparently, he had made quite a cake of himself. Though Rose hadn't been there to witness it for herself, she had heard all about it over the years.

"But if he hadn't lost the bet, he might never have wed you," she pointed out.

The terms of the bet indicated that if Griffin and his friends lost, Lord Danford would be allowed to dictate who they would wed as punishment. After successfully getting Lady Gillian to fall in love with him, Lord Danford chose Adel to be Griffin's wife. Of course, he only did it because he could tell that Griffin was already very much enamored with her, and the two did end up falling in love in the end.

"Oh, I'm certain he would still have wed me," Adel said confidently as she looked over at her husband who was sitting in a chair next to the bed, a faraway look on his face. "Right, Griffin?"

When he failed to answer, Rose called out, "Griffin, are you listening to a word we say?"

No answer.

Adel threw another antique article of clothing atop the pile and went to her husband, placing a hand gently on his shoulder. "Sweetheart, what is wrong? You have been strangely aloof since your return."

Rose waited anxiously to hear if her brother would finally admit the truth to Adel, for she still didn't know what his hasty trip to London had truly been about. Rose could understand that he didn't want her to worry, but what he failed to see was that his strange behavior was more concerning to her than the truth would be.

Placing one hand atop hers, he snapped out of his reverie and looked up at his wife, the love he had for her so evident in the silent exchange of words that took place in that brief glance. "I'm sorry, my love. I have a lot on my mind, my father's unexpected death not the least of them. And going through all of his belongings is getting quite tedious."

"We can always have the servants see to the rest."

"Yes, as soon as we finish in here, I think that is what we will do. I just didn't want them throwing out anything that could have held sentimental value."

Rose laughed at that comment, though it held no mirth. "We all know that anything belonging to father does not hold any sentiment to either of us."

"But there are several of mother's things in here as well."

"Yes, but all of her valuable or sentimental items have long since been cleared. Her jewelry is locked up and kept safe. Are you looking for something in particular?"

Griffin's shoulders drooped perceptibly. "No, I suppose I am not." He gave his wife's hand a gentle squeeze and said, "Go rest a bit. I will finish up here and then go check on the children."

Adel yawned loudly, "That sounds like a fine idea."

As soon as she quit the room, Rose turned to Griffin. "What is it you're looking for?"

"I've been foolishly hoping to find a clue," he said as he ran one hand nervously through his hair.

"To father's murder? Do you suppose we would be astute enough to find something that Andrew, a professional, had missed?"

"I didn't think so, but I had a sliver of hope. I feel so helpless, sitting here awaiting word from Cameron. I wish he would have let me help investigate."

Upon his return, Griffin had made her fully aware of Cameron's involvement. She was beyond grateful that he had not divulged the fact to her brother that he was also trying to clear the suspicion that surrounded her as well. She was certain that Griffin would have a fit if he knew she was suspected of a string of murders.

"You need to trust that he will do his job. It is better that you are here with us. Adel would not be pleased with your extended absence."

Just then, Prince came bounding into the room and headed straight for Griffin, licking his face as if he were cleaning up a newborn pup. Rose laughed at the disgust that was evident on Griffin's face. "I think it's safe to say that Prince would not be pleased with your extended absence either."

Griffin glared at her. "Get this beast away from me."

"You have more strength than me. If you cannot put him away from your person, I will not be successful either."

"That's not funny, Rose. You know all you have to do is call him, and he'll come. Now do it."

"Did you hear that?" she asked as she cocked her ear towards the door. "I think I hear Adel calling me. Sorry, but I must be off." Lifting the worn skirt of her old gown into her hands, Rose scampered off before her brother could chastise her in a way that would offend her sensibilities.

As soon as she reached her bedchamber, she rang for her maid who was there at once. She instructed her to help her from the worn and faded dress she had worn to sort through her father's belongings into a pale blue cotton day dress sprigged with flowers. She was sitting at her dressing table while her maid arranged her hair into a simple chignon when Griffin stormed into the room, without even knocking. He held a piece of parchment in his hand.

"I should throttle you for leaving me alone with that mutt," he spat, still clearly upset about what she had just done. "But I will taunt you with this instead." Holding the letter up before him he said, "I just received word from Lord deCourtenay."

Rose sprang from her seat, nearly knocking her maid over. "What does he say?" she asked anxiously as she rushed across the room to where he was standing.

"Wouldn't you like to know?"

He held the letter high above her head, just out of reach. "Tell me what he said, Griffin."

"Nope. If you want to know, you'll have to read it yourself."

She stood on tip-toe in an attempt to reach the letter, but he only held it higher out of reach. "You're being cruel," she accused.

"No crueler than you were to me. I have half a mind to send that beast of a dog packing."

"You wouldn't." Though she was appalled, she kept trying to reach for the letter he dangled above her, just out of reach.

"If he ever licks my face like that again, I can assure you that I will indeed find him a new home."

"Don't be ridiculous; he always licks you."

"And I have always hated it."

Rolling back on her heels, Rose stopped reaching for the letter. Instead, she folded her arms across her chest and said defiantly, "If you do not give me that letter, I will tell Adel that you are investigating father's murder."

"Your threat won't work with me," he laughed as he tweaked her nose. "I had already told her myself before I came to see you."

"You're lying."

Ignoring her accusation, he lowered the letter a bit and said, "Promise me you will never leave me to that dog's unholy ministrations ever again, and I will tell you what the letter says."

"Fine," she huffed, though she wasn't precisely sure how he expected her to keep that promise. "I agree. Now tell me what it says."

Lowering his arm, Griffin spoke without nary a glance at the letter. "Lord deCourtenay has obtained some information but did not want to risk anything by sending word in a letter that could easily have been lost or read. He has invited us to visit his family's estate where he can tell me what he has learned."

"Did he speak of me?" she asked hopefully.

"Of course he did. He insists that you come as well, for he misses your presence greatly."

Rose couldn't help herself, she squealed in delight. "When do we leave?"

"As soon as you can have your belongings readied."

"Well then I must insist you leave at once so I can see to the task," she said as she shooed him from the room, a broad smile plastered across her face.

Chapter Eighteen

The ride to Cameron's family estate took nearly two full days of travel, leaving Rose fairly exhausted by the time the carriage pulled up to the large, stone estate. She wasn't sure what she expected, but the chill of foreboding that coursed up her spine as their carriage approached was not at all what she anticipated feeling.

She twisted her hands nervously, trying to rationalize why she felt so strange. She was certain it was because of her past experiences. She recalled all too well the first time her late husband took her to meet his family and it was not a pleasant visit. His aging and frail mother had looked her over intently before declaring her too thin to be of any value as a breeder. She had been shocked and offended by the lady's crude comment and even more shocked when her husband had slapped his mother for suggesting he did not make a good selection.

"What if they don't like me?" her weak voice sliced through the silence in the carriage.

Griffin's head was resting against the side of the carriage, his eyes closed, though Rose knew he wasn't asleep. He lifted his head slowly as he rubbed one hand across his stubbled jaw. "Of course they will like you."

"The Moncrief's didn't."

"Rose," he said patiently, his voice holding a hint of tenderness, "Lord deCourtenay is a completely different man than the baron. I do not think he would have invited you here to meet his family if he thought they would treat you horribly. I am certain everything will be fine."

All she could do was shake her head and hope that he was right.

Rose spent the remainder of the ride glancing out the window, taking in her surroundings. The land surrounding the estate was free of any trees or shrubbery, making it appear rather bland. The only thing that broke up the monotony of the landscape was a large outbuilding to the left of the house that appeared as if it were possibly a hothouse.

As the carriage approached the house, Rose was surprised that no line of footman formed to greet them. "Are you sure this is the right place?"

"I gave Lord deCourtenay's directions to the driver."

As the carriage rolled to a stop, Rose took a fortifying breath as Griffin alighted from the carriage then turned to assist her. She tried to quell her apprehension by reminding herself that any minute now she would be seeing Cameron. The thought of gazing into his intense eyes made her momentarily forget her insecurities and allowed her to walk arm in arm with Griffin to the front door.

As the butler opened the door, the first thought Rose had was that the man must be dead. His skin was ashen, and his cheeks were hollow. The pasty skin on his face and hands seemed to drip from his bones, and Rose could have sworn he smelled like a decaying corpse as well, though she wasn't entirely sure what that smelled like.

"We have been waiting for you," his low voice drawled as he showed them inside.

Rose shivered as she entered. The house was drafty and devoid of any décor that would make it feel homely. She and Griffin exchanged a confused look as they followed the butler, ever so slowly, to the drawing room.

"Wait in here," was all he said as he turned and shut the door, making Rose feel trapped.

"Something doesn't feel right," she whispered to Griffin, both of them refusing to sit.

"It is a bit...strange. Perhaps only because our expectations have not been met. I anticipated something quite different."

"Me too," she admitted.

Neither one of them spoke another word as they waited. Rose wished desperately that Cameron would hurry and make an appearance and cut through the frosty stillness that enshrouded them. She was greatly disappointed when the door opened to reveal the butler once more.

"I regret to inform you that Lord deCourtenay has yet to arrive. I have been instructed to show you to your bedchambers. The servants have already delivered your trunks."

Disappointment engulfed Rose as they once more found themselves following the sluggish butler to the second floor where their chambers were located. Rose was shown to her bedchamber first. She reluctantly bid Griffin goodbye as the butler informed them that dinner would be served in two hours.

The room was just as impersonal as the rest of the house was. It was adorned in the barest of furnishings, and there was no fire lit in the hearth. Shivering once more, Rose went and unlatched her trunk, hoping to find a pelisse to put on over her dress to warm her. Rummaging through her belongings, she suddenly wondered where her maid was and why she wasn't in here unpacking her trunk.

Alas, Rose was used to doing things for herself since she'd had to fend for herself for so many years and began at once to unpack her belongings. The rustling of fabrics was the only sound in the room and the silence was beginning to feel suffocating.

With her trunk unpacked and her clothes hanging neatly in the armoire, Rose didn't know what to do with herself. She sat on the edge of the bed and reached for the heart-shaped locket hanging around her neck. The gold felt warm from resting against her skin, and she took a moment to simply hold it, and revel in its warmth. It was the only thing that didn't feel cold at the moment. When her chilled hands had sucked all of the heat from the locket, she used her fingernail to pry it open and reverently took the folded piece of parchment from inside and opened it so she could read the poem Cameron had written her, though she had memorized it already. Oh, how she wished he would arrive soon.

The sound of the door opening startled Rose, causing her to drop the poem into her lap. She quickly retrieved it and replaced it back inside the locket before glancing to the elderly woman standing in the doorway. Why did everyone here appear to be half dead?

"I came to help dress you for dinner, my lady."

"Where is my maid?" she asked curtly.

Ignoring her question, the woman moved into the room. Rose turned and watched her shuffle to the armoire and begin rummaging through her clothing. Her gnarled hands inspected every dress before she turned to Rose and said disdainfully, "None of these will do. I will return shortly."

Rose stood rooted in her place, her mouth hanging open in shock. She wanted to rush from the room and find Griffin, but she didn't know where to look. When the woman returned, she held an aging white muslin dress over her arm. She went and laid it reverently atop the coverpane.

Rose inspected the dress, noticing the ribbons were yellowing from age. Her eyes squinted as she stepped forward to get a better look. Her fingers slid gently over the fabric as she lifted one sleeve and gasped as her eyes settled upon a dark stain on the underside of the cuff.

"Where did you get this dress?"

"From the master. Now hurry and let me dress you or you will be late for dinner, and the master will not be pleased."

Rose felt her chest tightening, squeezing the air from her lungs. Perhaps she was wrong; perhaps this wasn't the dress from her childhood, the same dress she had ruined when she accidentally dipped her sleeve into her hot chocolate at breakfast.

"That won't fit me." It was the only thing she could think to say as her mind was reeling and she couldn't make sense of what was happening.

The woman's gray eyes turned stormy, her lips pinching tightly together in displeasure. "Trust me; you will regret not obeying the master."

Rose shook her head, backing away from the bed. This had to be some sort of nightmare, and soon, very soon, she'd wake up. "Is Lord deCourtenay here?" she asked hopefully, though her voice was shakey.

"The master will not be pleased," the woman scolded, not answering her question.

Rose kept backing up, unwilling to do anything the lady wanted. By now she was certain this was a nightmare, and she refused to participate. As soon as she turned the knob on the door, the woman reached for the bell pull and tugged violently. Rose turned and fled, slamming the door behind her.

Where was Griffin? She ran from room to room, opening each door and calling his name, not caring if she encountered anyone else. She had to find her brother and tell him that she wished to leave. Her whole body was shaking violently as she pushed another door open and glanced in. This bedchamber was more elaborately decorated than any other she had been in, and the roaring fire in the hearth momentarily beckoned her inward.

"Griffin," her voice broke as she skittishly advanced into the room. "Are you in here?"

"Who is there?" an oddly pleasant voice called out behind the thick velvet drapes that hung from the canopied bed.

Her breath hitched as her feet stilled, refusing to go any further.

"Come, tell me who you are, my child, and what you are doing in my bedchamber."

Rose somehow found her voice. "My apologies, I didn't mean to intrude. I was merely looking for my brother."

"Who is your brother, dear?"

She moved closer, hoping to get a look at the lady speaking as she said, "Lord Straton."

"Unfortunately, I have yet to meet him. Come here, dear, and let me get a better look at you."

If it weren't for the kindness in her voice, Rose would never have done as she bade. As she approached the bed, all she could see was a head full of gray hair topped with a mobcap nestled among the pillows. The woman smiled widely at her, and Rose couldn't help smiling back.

"Who are you?" Rose was curious to know.

"I am the master's mother. I would ask who you are, but there's no need for that, for I already know you must be his love. You are as beautiful as he claimed you'd be."

For the first time since arriving, Rose felt hopeful. "Is Lord deCourtenay here then? I have been waiting to see him."

Ignoring her question, the woman cooed, "So, so beautiful. I can understand his obsession."

"Where is your son?"

"Waiting for you at dinner. Why aren't you dressed?"

Rose sighed, "I wanted to find my brother."

"He is waiting for you as well, dear. Go, get dressed and join them."

The woman's eyes were so kind. "Will you be joining us?"

"Me? Oh no, I am not well enough for that. Go, enjoy yourself. My son has a splendid surprise waiting for you."

Rose felt conflicted as she walked back to her bedchamber. Things had felt so strange, so wrong, but then she met Cameron's mother and the lady was somehow able to put her at ease a bit, at least until she returned to her bedchamber and found the same woman still there, still insisting she wear her old dress.

"If you do not put this on, I am instructed not to allow you to leave your bedchamber."

"How will you keep me here?"

"By force, if necessary."

Rose eyed the woman, who was much shorter than her but quite a bit larger, and wondered if she'd really be able to keep her from leaving. With great reluctance, she finally decided just to put the dress on so she could go down to dinner and see Cameron and Griffin and find out why things felt so strange here.

Chapter Nineteen

Rose felt ridiculous clad in the too tight dress of her childhood. The bodice was squeezing the air from her lungs, making it hard to breathe. She feared if she moved too quickly she would rip a seam, so though she was anxious to get to dinner, to be around Cameron and Griffin and feel some sense of normalcy, her steps were slow and deliberate.

The same old woman who had dressed her was now showing her to the dining room. Her heart beat wildly with anticipation as she was shown into a narrow room with a long table directly in the center. There were hundreds of candles scattered about, all lit, but instead of making the room bright and inviting, they only served to cast eery shadows in every direction as their flames danced wildly as if there was a draft, though the room felt oddly still.

Rose's eyes settled on the table where only one place setting was set. She turned to ask the woman about it and realized that the old lady had left. She was completely alone in the room; her brows scrunched together in confusion.

Her head whipped around as the loud scraping of a chair echoed off the high ceiling, causing her to startle.

"Come, sit," the butler commanded as his bony hand gestured to the chair in front of him.

Rose hesitated. "Where's Lord deCourtenay? Where is my brother?"

"They have not arrived yet. Come, be seated so dinner may begin."

Doing as she was told, Rose sat stiffly in the chair and watched as a footman scurried from the shadows, a serving bowl of soup in his hands. Without saying a word, he ladled the steaming liquid into her bowl, then disappeared as fast as he had appeared.

"Am I to eat alone?" she asked before realizing she had been left alone once more.

Staring at the steam rising from her soup, Rose wondered about the oddness that was surrounding her. She waited several moments, hoping that someone would appear, that Cameron and Griffin would arrive so things could return to normal. When nothing but silence greeted her, she began to lose hope, and her heart plummeted in despair. What was she to do?

"Eat, or you will not have the strength that you need."

Rose couldn't see the butler, only hear his monotone voice coming from somewhere behind her. She didn't voice an answer, just sat and stared at the cooling soup, refusing to touch it.

"Perhaps the soup is not to your liking? Samuel, clear the soup."

The footman returned, scooping up the soup from before her before disappearing into the shadows. Rose simply stared at the empty spot before her, wondering what would happen next. She didn't have to wait long, for the footman returned swiftly, this time carrying a silver platter covered with a lid. He set the platter before her, the domed cover reaching up to her forehead. She stared at the dish, momentarily distracted as she wondered what it could contain.

"Perhaps this will be more to your liking," the butler's voice intoned behind her.

The footman reached forth and with a flourish removed the cover revealing a pineapple. Rose gasped as she bolted from her seat, backing away from the fruit, her mind racing furiously. She contemplated leaving the house and finding her way to the stables and demanding her driver return her to Manhall Manor at once. Something was not right here, she could feel it in her bones.

The only problem that seemed to oppose that plan was the fact that she was frozen in place, unable to move. Fear was slithering through her body, wrapping it's tentacles firmly around her limbs. She felt as if a thick cloud of darkness was about to consume her. Was Cameron playing a game with her? Did he find this amusing, because she certainly didn't?

In her state of shock, she didn't realize that someone was approaching until she felt two hands settle firmly on her shoulders. She gasped in shock and tried to turn, but the person held her in place.

"The master is waiting for you. Let us go to him now."

Surprisingly, the butler was stronger than he appeared. His solid grip on her shoulders was unrelenting as he pushed her forward, directing her where he wanted her to go. Past the long table they went, out the door at the other end of the dining room and on down the drafty hall that eventually led them to the foyer. One bony hand let go of her shoulder long enough to open the door before it returned to its place and began pushing her out into the cold night.

Rose shivered as they moved onward, the butler never shutting the door behind them. With the faintest of hope, she wondered if it were possible that the man might truly be leading her to Cameron. She tried to reach deep within herself to find and hold onto that faint glimmer as he propelled her forward through the thick grass that was wet from an earlier rainstorm. She fought to stay upright as her slippers slid in the wet grass as they hurried along towards the Hothouse Rose noticed upon their arrival.

There was such a contrast between the chilly air outside and the hot, muggy air inside the building it nearly suffocated Rose as she was forced inside.

"She is here," the butler called out as he pushed her inside, causing her to trip and fall to the ground.

Rose called out in pain as her knees hit the hard ground below, her hands instantly going forward to catch herself. She cringed as they encountered something sticky and she gasped in alarm as she noticed a dark stain beneath her palms. Pulling them back as if they had been burned, she turned them over and gasped as the metallic scent of blood filled her nostrils. Rose felt her head begin to swim and she was sure she was going to swoon.

"Ah, the princess has arrived," an unfamiliar man's voice purred from somewhere in the darkness.

Rose's head snapped up as she glanced around, noticing for the first time the rows and rows of spiky green pineapple crowns poking through the soil. This wasn't an ordinary hothouse.

As if the man could read her mind, he asked, "Do you like my pinerie? It has proven to be quite the lucrative business. The Earl of Danford heard of my success and sent his man of affairs out to discuss the possibility of investing in my operation."

Rose's ears perked up at the sound of a familiar name. "Is Lord Danford here?" she asked hopefully.

The man laughed dryly before continuing, "Unfortunately for him; I knew the real purpose of his visit was to investigate me, not my business, and that would not do."

"What are you talking about?"

"Your brother thinks I am responsible for your father's death."

"Who are you?" she called out, her eyes looking frantically around, trying to find out who this man was she was trapped with.

"I'm hurt you don't recognize my voice," he answered sadly. "Alas, it has changed since my boyhood. But you," he cooed as his voice drew closer, "have not changed a bit. You are just as beautiful as you've always been."

Rose cried out as a strong arm snaked around her middle and lifted her from the floor, cradling her body against a solid chest. She felt the man's face nuzzle into her neck and she wanted to cast up her accounts.

"You smell like heaven." How he could smell anything past the stench of manure that permeated the room was beyond her.

Through trembling lips, she managed to ask, "Who are you?"

"Jasper, my pet. I'm wounded that you still do not recognize me."

"Well perhaps if I could see your face I would."

With a surprising gentleness, he turned her in his arms, so she was facing him. "Jasper Howe? My mother's cousin?" A delighted smile spread across his vaguely familiar face. It had been many, many years since she had seen him or thought of him.

"Yes, your mother's cousin, and soon to be your husband."

"No, you must be confused, I am to wed Lord deCourtenay."

"You can't marry a dead man," he stated coldly, and Rose's blood ran chill. The crusted blood on her hands seemed to singe through her skin. Was it Cameron's blood?

"Where is he?" she hissed, a panic unlike any she had ever before experienced consuming her. Pushing her stained hands against his chest, she tried to pull away and escape his embrace. "Where is he? Tell me where he is, right now. Please," she begged as sobs overtook her body, "tell me where he is."

"I do not like seeing you make yourself hysterical over that undeserving fool. He hasn't loved you since his childhood like I have. Forget about him; there is only me now."

Jasper swept her into his arms, cradling her like a child as he began to move towards the door. Rose kicked her legs wildly, though the tight skirt of her dress greatly restricted her movement as she used one hand to reach up and claw viciously at his face.

Instead of dropping her as she had hoped, he shook her angrily as he hissed, "Do that to me again, and you will regret it."

Rose was already regretting it as he continued shaking her, making her feel as if her neck would snap. "I have ways of getting you to behave how I wish, though I'd much prefer it if you'd just behave like the sweet Rose that I remember you being. My sweet, sweet Rose."

Finally, the shaking stopped, and he was once more holding her against his chest, stroking her hair in an odd attempt to calm her. His actions did not soothe her, just frightened her immensely. Rose felt weak as her head throbbed angrily. She had to try and ignore the pain and think of a way to escape.

"We will be wed tonight. In a moments time, you will be mine forever. There's no one who can deny me my wish now."

Rose thought back to her father's death and couldn't help but ask, "Did you kill him?"

His shoulders shrugged nonchalantly. "I've killed lots of people. I was a General in the war, after all."

"My father," she spat out. "Did you kill my father?"

"I had to," he said without apology. "He wouldn't let me wed you. Now, there is no one standing in my way.

"Griffin will never give you permission to wed me."

"Griffin, your brother?" he asked through a hearty laugh. "I don't see him here trying to stop me."

"Where is he?" she asked, knowing he knew exactly where he was.

"You have too many questions, my pet. The only thing I want you thinking about is me. Stop asking me about these other men. It makes me very, very unhappy." He spoke slowly as if he were explaining something complex to a simple-minded child. "Now, let us go. We have a wedding to attend."

Rose wasn't sure how she was going to stop it, but she knew that there was no way she was going to marry this man. She'd let him kill her first. Besides, if Cameron was dead, she had no reason to go on living anyways.

Rose tried to swat at Jasper's wandering hands as he carried her inside the house and up to her bedchamber but he was much too strong, and her protests did nothing to stop him. He kept pawing at her as he proclaimed his love for her over and over, expressing his eagerness to wed her that very night.

As soon as they reached her bedchamber, he deposited her gently on the bed and said, "Your maid will dress you for the ceremony while I go freshen up. The next time I see you, you will be mine, all mine."

Rose shook her head and managed to squeak out a weak, "No."

Jasper froze, his blue eyes turning to ice. He reached out and struck her across the face. "Don't ever tell me no again, do you understand?"

Her head snapped back with the force of the blow, her skin stinging where his palm made contact. It had been so long since she had been hit by a man, but memories of the abuse her late husband inflicted upon her came rushing back as if it had occurred yesterday.

Rose bit down on her cheek in an effort to stop her sobs from escaping, but it was no use. A strangled sob escaped, and she was worried she'd be hit again. Instead, Jasper dropped on his knees next to the bed and gathered her into his arms, the same hand he used to strike her was now stroking her hair, her cheek, as he whispered fervent apologies in her ear.

"My pet, you make me do irrational things. I can't think straight when I'm around you. Please forgive me, but I confess I do everything only with your best interest in mind. You will not be happy if you continue telling me no, if you keep resisting me. Submit yourself to me, and I can assure you we will be wildly happy together. Just you wait and see."

This man was crazy; Rose thought as she held still in his arms, afraid to defy him and make him angry again, though his touch made her skin crawl and her stomach revolt. She had to get away from him, from this place. Her silence seemed to satisfy him for the moment, and he left, with the promise to see her shortly.

As soon as she was alone, Rose ran to the window and opened it, glancing at the ground below, judging if she could jump without hurting herself. She knew it would be insane to do, but it was her only hope for escape. She bent over and tugged on the hem of her tight skirt, ripping it up the middle so she could swing her leg up over the ledge. She was straddling the windowsill, about to jump when she felt strong hands pull her back, causing her to fall into the room on top of somebody. Her plan had been thwarted.

Chapter Twenty

Cameron held his breath as he twisted the handle and opened the door that led to the servants quarters. He had been riding at a furious pace for an entire day to get to Bedfordshire in record time. He had left for Manhall Manor as soon as he heard from Lord Danford that his man of affairs had departed for Bedfordshire. Upon his arrival, Lady Adel had informed him that Rose and Lord Straton had gone to visit him at his family estate in Bedfordshire, upon his request. She was greatly confused to see him. He knew at once that something was amiss.

He whispered a silent prayer that he wasn't too late as he slid quietly into the dim halls of the manor house, hoping he could find Rose before someone detected his presence. The servants quarters was oddly quiet. There was no one to be found in the kitchen and no evidence of dinner being prepared and served. In fact, the only sound he could hear was a low, repetitive pounding as if someone was knocking on a door.

His eyes glanced around, wondering who was making the noise when his eyes settled on the closed door of what must surely be the wine cellar. He rushed to it and attempted to force the door open, but it was locked. The knocking got louder. Someone was behind that door. Was it Rose?

"Stand back," he warned as he kicked the door handle hoping to break it loose. When that failed to work, he glanced around the room until he noticed a heavy cast iron pan hanging from a hook. He ran and grabbed it then used it to bang against the door handle until the knob broke and the door swung open. Lying on the floor not far from the door was Lord Straton, his arms tied tightly behind his back and a cravat binding his mouth.

Cameron dropped to the floor and swiftly cut the ropes that were binding him. As soon as he freed him, he asked, "What is going on here?"

Lord Straton rubbed the knot on his forehead where he had banged it repeatedly against the door hoping to garner someone's attention. "General Howe has Rose. We've got to find them."

Though he had so many questions, he refused to waste any more time asking them. Instead, he helped Lord Straton to his feet and slid the small dagger into his palm. "Take this. For your protection."

"But what about you?"

He patted his chest. "I have a pistol in here." Lord Straton nodded his head in admiration, then signaled him to lead them along.

Cameron had no idea where he was going, but an urgency to save and protect Rose compelled him forward. His pace was swift as he jogged up the stairs leading to the main level. "Rose," he called out loudly as he searched furiously behind every closed door.

Lord Straton worked with him, looking frantically for his sister as he too called out her name, hoping she would hear them and yell back, but they were only met with silence.

"Let's check the bedchambers," Cameron suggested, already on his way towards the next flight of stairs. "She's got to be here somewhere."

"Wait," Lord Straton called out behind him, causing Cameron to pause. "Perhaps she is not in the house." Cameron eyed him quizzically. "Perhaps she is in one of the outbuildings."

Cameron instantly thought of the pinerie and quickly nodded his head. "Yes, you're right. Let's split up and look for her. Time is of the utmost importance right now."

"I'll go outside; you keep looking in here." Cameron nodded then watched as Lord Straton jogged back down the stairs before he resumed his search. One of them better find her, and quick.

Cameron was beginning to wonder if he should have gone to look outside when he heard footsteps behind him and turned to see a petite, mousy looking maid approaching.

"I've been waiting for you," she said as she drew near.

Cameron looked at her quizzically. "You've been looking for me?"

"Yes." Grabbing onto his arm, she began tugging him forward. When he dug the heels of his boots into the rug and refused to move, she gave him a knowing look and said, "I know where Rose is. I'm only trying to take you to her."

The mention of Rose made him follow the girl who had already begun walking. He had to jog a few paces to keep up with her departing figure as she moved swiftly down the hall, stopping only once she approached the bedchamber that he assumed held Rose prisoner.

Instead of knocking, however, the maid pushed the door open and at once ran inside. Cameron moved swiftly into the room and watched as the small girl dove for the window where he glanced in shock and saw Rose, half her body hanging out, about to jump. His heart beat frantically as he watched the maid pull her forcefully back inside, the two of them falling to the ground with a loud thump.

He ran to Rose, scooping her into his arms, so grateful to see her alive. She clung to him furiously as tears streamed from her eyes. "Cameron, I thought you were dead. The blood in the pinerie," she said as she held up her dirtied palms so he could see, "I thought it was yours."

"No, my love, I am safe. We are safe, and I'm getting you away from here right now."

He made to leave, but the maid rushed to the door and threw her body in front of it in an attempt to block them. He almost laughed aloud, knowing there was no way she could stop him, that is until she pulled a pistol from the pocket of her gown and pointed it directly at them. He stilled.

"Oh no, you're not going anywhere."

"Esther, what is the meaning of this?" Rose asked.

"Esther?" he asked her. "The maid who betrayed you." Rose simply nodded her head.

"I've waited a long time for this moment. I have spent years plotting the perfect revenge, and it was going quite well, but I think I like this ending even better."

"What do you mean? What revenge?"

A satisfied smile made Esther appear rather wicked as she kept the pistol trained on them and explained, "Your husband and I were lovers. You foolishly thought I stayed with you because of my affection for you, but it was my love for him that kept me there. You betrayed him by mentioning his debts to the gossip rags, embarrassing him so."

"That's why you allowed him to beat me? You thought it was I who reported him to the columns? Esther, I didn't do it."

Ignoring her, Esther continued, "He was going to divorce you and marry me."

Cameron interjected, "Impossible. A baron would not divorce a lady of the ton to wed a servant."

Fire flashed in Esther's eyes. "He was going to do it, he promised me," she hissed. "But it never happened because she," Esther pointed the gun directly at Rose, "killed him."

"He killed himself!" Rose wailed. "I had nothing to do with his death."

"You made his life so miserable; he felt he had no other choice. It's all your fault. That is why I have meticulously carried out my plan, in hopes of destroying your life as you have destroyed so many others."

Cameron squinted at the girl as his mind raced and things began clicking into place. "You!" he exclaimed a bit loudly, causing Rose to startle in his arms. "You are the one who has been killing the men of the *ton*, making it appear as if Rose is the person responsible for those deaths."

"Too bad you couldn't have figured that out before now."

"Is General Howe in on this as well?" Cameron asked.

"Oh no, this is all my doing. He came to collect on what the baron owed him and that is when he learned of his death. I had no place to go, and the dear man took me in, offering me a position selling pineapples. It was the perfect way to get into the homes of the men I needed dead. No one suspected a lowly maid delivering pineapple of murder. His kindness saved his life, for I was unwilling to kill a man that showed me so much generosity."

"Did you kill her father as well?" Cameron asked, not aware that General Howe had already admitted to Rose that it had been he who had done it.

"No, that was all the General's doing, though I did tell him the best way to kill him. Poison. It's much, much cleaner, though I don't suspect I could get either of you to drink some now, could I? No matter, this will prove just as effective."

Cameron knew it was coming and just as her finger pulled the trigger, he threw Rose to the ground, landing next to her on the floor. The ball swooshed above them, implanting into the wall behind them.

Esther cursed then furiously began working to reload the pistol, but

Cameron had retrieved his pistol by then and was now pointing it at her. "Drop the pistol and I'll spare your life."

"And leave me to the gallows instead? I think not."

Cameron had no other choice. She finished loading the pistol and just as her finger grazed the trigger, he shot, his aim perfect. Esther crumpled to the floor, blood oozing out of her chest. Beside him, Rose let out a sob. Cameron went to her, grabbing her once more into his arms.

"I'm sorry you had to witness that, my love. I'm so, so sorry." She was shaking, and it hurt Cameron to see her so frightened. "She would have killed you and I could not have lived with myself had I allowed that to happen."

"I had no idea she hated me so badly. She's been trying to destroy me for years. What if she had been successful?"

Cameron shuddered at the thought, knowing how close she had been to succeeding. "I wouldn't have let that happen," he whispered as he stroked her cheek, just now noticing the purplish bruise that marred her face. "What happened here?" his voice was full of concern as he gently trailed his fingers across her cheekbone.

"Jasper did it." Her lip trembled and he couldn't help placing his own lips atop them. Leaning forward he kissed her gently, though he wanted nothing more than to consume her with his love. She was safe now and she was his.

Her trembling stopped as he kissed her and whispered, "Rose, I love you and I always promise to keep you safe."

"Yes, and you have." She clung to him and he rather liked the feel of her slight body pressed against him.

He couldn't resist asking, "Have I earned your love yet?" He knew it probably wasn't fair for him to pry, especially in such tender circumstances, but he had to know, had to hear it from her own lips.

But alas, it wasn't mean to be, for right at that moment, they were interrupted by an angry voice, "Who killed my servant?"

"It's Jasper," Rose cried. "He'll kill you."

"No, he won't," he said confidently as he once more reached for his pistol.

"Yes, I will," he hollered as he stepped over Esther's lifeless body, waving his own pistol furiously in front of him. "Why did you kill my servant and why are you touching my bride?"

"I'll never be your bride," Rose hollered. "I'm marrying Lord deCourtenay. And besides, I could never wed a man who killed my own father."

The General's otherwise handsome face distorted into anger as he lunged for Rose, "I killed your mother as well. Spooked her horse while she was out riding."

Rose's face went white. "How could you? My mother would never harm a soul."

"Except for me. She refused to let me have you. You know how I feel about people telling me no." Yes, she had an angry, painful bruise on her cheek to remind her.

"Now come here, my pet. The priest is waiting to wed us."

"Touch her and you'll die," Cameron threatened, pointing the pistol at him.

194

General Howe paused for only a moment before scooping Rose into his arms. Cameron pulled the trigger but nothing happened. He hadn't had time to reload the ball. Cursing, he threw the pistol aside. General Howe turned to leave, holding Rose in his arms. Cameron threw his arm around his neck, grabbing him in a choke-hold. He ripped his head backwards, the crook of his elbow digging into his Adam's apple, trapping the air from reaching his lungs.

"Drop her," he commanded, tightening his hold.

Refusing to do as he bid, General Howe kicked his foot backward into Cameron's shin, causing a sharp pain to shoot through his leg. Cameron's lips tightened together as he twisted his arm, forcing General Howe's neck painfully to one side. He cried out and released Rose as his arms went up to try and pry Cameron's arm from off of his neck.

He scratched furiously at Cameron's arms, causing bloody scratches to appear, but he refused to let go of him. Instead, Cameron kept tightening his grip, hoping that he would pass out soon from lack of air.

All of a sudden, General How cried out in agony and crumpled to the ground. Cameron looked down and saw that Rose was holding a bloody dagger. "Where did you get that?" he asked in awe.

Rose smiled proudly, "I saw it poking out of the top of his boot. When he dropped me, I reached for it and stabbed him in the leg."

Sure enough, General Howe was writhing in pain, clinging to the spot on his leg that was bleeding profusely.

"What are we going to do now?" Rose asked as she came and stood beside him.

"We will keep this bastard locked up while we send for the authorities."

Rose and Cameron's heads snapped towards the door where Griffin was standing, his large frame taking up the entire entry.

"Griffin, you're alive!" Rose flung herself into his arms.

"Yes, though I cannot say the same for Benedict's man of affairs. I found his dead body in the pinerie."

"That's who's blood I felt," Rose stated sadly as she looked at her still dirtied palms. "I need a bath."

"Yes, and we will get that arranged as soon as we get things taken care of here."

"He killed both Father and Mother," Rose looked as if she would cry as she told her brother what she had learned.

"Yes, I suspected as much. Did he confess?"

"He did," Cameron answered. "Both Rose and I can bear witness of his confession to the authorities."

"Very good." Then, leaning over the squirming body of General Howe, Lord Straton spit vehemently, "You've ruined your life, *cousin*, just like you've ruined so many others. I hope you rot in hell." Then, he turned to Cameron and said, "Let's lock him in here while we send for the authorities. I can't stand to look at the man responsible for my parent's death a minute longer."

As they were making to leave the room, Lord Straton seemed to notice Esther's dead body for the first time. "What is this about?" he asked, one dark brow cocked curiously.

Cameron sighed, "I will explain it all to you shortly. It's quite a long story. For now, let's get Rose away from this carnage."

"There is nothing that would please me more."

Epilogue

Rose rested her head against Cameron's shoulder, one hand petting Prince's head that was lying in her lap as the carriage rolled along, heading towards Manhall Manor. It had been almost two months since they had wed, and Rose had never been happier. As soon as they had received word from Griffin that Adel had given birth to a precious, and much-anticipated daughter, they had packed their belongings and left at once for a visit.

A smile formed on her lips as she watched Cameron's fingers stroking her palm. "I never told you why I gave Prince that name."

Cameron reached over and scratched behind the dog's ears. "Why is it you call him Prince? Is it because he acts like royalty?"

"No."

"Or is it because he's as large as Prinny himself?"

Rose giggled. "I already told you he wasn't named after the Prince Regent."

"Well then, I have run out of guesses."

"I named him after you."

"Me?" he asked curiously, as he shifted in his seat so he could look her in the eyes. "I don't understand."

"The night I got him I had a dream that I was a princess locked away in a tower, drowning in sorrow and unable to erase the ugly scars of my past from me. You showed up, my dashing prince, ready to rescue me, to save me. You made me forget all about the ugliness of my life and made my future seem bright. But when I awoke, I was all alone, save for him," she glanced down at Prince, resting obliviously in her lap.

Cameron reached forth and tilted her chin up so that she was looking at him. "Has your dream been fulfilled?"

Rose stared into his eyes, eyes so familiar they felt like she was home whenever she looked into them. "Yes, in so many ways. I never thought I would find love and now that I have, I can't remember how dreary my existence was without it."

"You've saved me too, you know?"

"I have? From what?"

"From myself. I was so wrapped up in my own pursuits, I didn't have time for anything or anyone and I most definitely didn't think I needed love and companionship. Oh, how I was wrong. If it weren't for you, I'd be working for the Main Office still, putting my life in danger and not caring one whit what happened to me, for I had nothing to live for. Now, I have a purpose. Now I have you."

Rose's eyes fluttered closed as she sighed and pressed her cheek into his palm. Andrew had apologized profusely for letting him off the case when he solved it and brought the true murderer to justice, as well as exposing another killer. He had nearly begged him to stay on as a secret agent, but Cameron had refused. It wasn't worth it to him anymore, and Rose had been relieved. As much as she admired his work, she wanted him home and safe with her.

"And soon you will have a child as well."

Cameron's hand jerked back from her face. "Rose, what are you saying?"

Her cheeks flushed with heat as she whispered softly, "I am with child."

"Are you certain?"

She nodded. "I have been with child enough times to be able to recognize the signs. I am positive."

Cameron squinted his eyes as he observed her as if he wasn't sure what she was saying was true. When he finally decided he could believe it, he scooped her into his arms, crushing her against his chest. Rose laughed as he clung to her. "I promise you will have the best care and get all the rest that you need. This baby is going to make it."

"And what if it doesn't," she had to ask.

His long fingers found her neck as he tilted her head back to look into his face. "Then I will hold you, and we will cry together, but we will never stop loving each other. My love and respect for you are not based on your ability to produce a child."

His lips found hers, and she instantly responded to the press of his tongue, opening her mouth to him. She was amazed at how much passion he produced in her, something she hadn't ever realized she possessed until he awakened it so fully inside of her. She would never stop wanting this husband of hers, and she was positively certain he would never stop wanting her. That knowledge had quite literally saved her, and she knew she'd never be the same.

The End

About The Author

Ginny Hartman has always loved writing, and when her love for the regency era blossomed, she decided to combine the two, resulting in her first published novel, *Deceiving the Duke of Kerrington*, which became an Amazon Historical Romance bestseller. After completing her first Regency Romance Trilogy, she decided to venture into other eras of historical romance, enjoying the journey back in time.

Ginny's favorite thing about writing is the escape it gives her and the people who read her stories. To be among the first to be notified when her new books are released, sign up for her newsletter at http://ginnyhartman.com/newsletter-sign-up. As an added bonus, you will also receive *Mrs. Tiddlyswan's Gossip Column,* an exclusive addition to Ginny's newsletter that will feature periodic updates on all of your favorite heroes and heroines. You can also like her Facebook page at https://www.facebook.com/authorginnyhartman.

Besides writing, Ginny enjoys reading and spending time with her favorite people: her husband and three beautiful children. She also enjoys traveling the world with the love of her life and gaining inspiration for her books. She currently resides in Northern Idaho.

Made in the USA
Charleston, SC
25 January 2017